A Man Out of Time

by N. Sullivan

First Print Edition 2014

ISBN: 0615971172

ISBN-13: 978-0615971179

Published by Sixty Six Underground

www.nsullivan.co

To my family, for everything.

To M.C. Shi[ley

CHAPTER 1

A map. Pittsburgh. It was tacked to a decaying, cracked, sick yellow-stained wall that had probably once been painted white, but hadn't been painted in a very long time. Two different colors of thumbtacks were stuck in the map. Red and black. Black strings led out along the wall in all directions from the black thumbtacks, eventually stopping at another thumbtack that was also holding up a newspaper clipping.

One black tack in the map was stuck directly into the heart of downtown, or as the locals called it, don-ton. The tack marked the location of a local lunch spot frequented by the movers and shakers who worked in the businesses that made their homes in the high rises that surrounded it. The black string tied to the tack led off to the right and ended in a small article, tacked near the corner of the room. The headline read Local Restaurant Robbed in Middle of Lunch Rush.

From the tack that held this article, three more black strings emanated. One led up, another straight down. The third turned the corner of the room and stretched about two thirds of the way along the right-hand wall and slightly downward, passing a pile of dirty clothes and a couple of empty suitcases, not to mention several more unrelated black strings, newspaper articles, and assorted stains of dubious origin along the way. This string ended just above a two foot stack of manila folders with Pittsburgh Police Department and Confidential boldly stamped on their covers and an equally tall stack of Styrofoam fast food containers that had become a home and breeding ground for every possible type of segmented-bodied vermin that modern city living had to offer while somehow managing to balance on a small, worn wooden table that had been in the same spot so long it might as well have been bolted to the floor but all the same shook and shimmied like drunken Jell-O every time a door slammed in the hall of the single room occupancy building.

The tack at the end of the string this time didn't end in a newspaper article. There was a bright white sheet of printed paper skewered to the wall here. It was a police rap sheet, complete with a picture of a surly looking middle aged white guy glaring out into the room. He didn't seem at all pleased to have his picture taken. Below the picture were all the vital statistics the police need to identify any hardened criminal: Age, weight, height, hair color, tattoos, mother's maiden name, blood type, mother's blood type, favorite band from the Eighties, how many licks he thinks it takes to get to the Tootsie Roll center of a Tootsie Pop, et cetera. At the bottom of the page, one word was highlighted: Deceased.

Two black strings and one in a disturbing shade of red were attached to the tack in the rap sheet. The red string cut straight across the room. One of the black strings led straight up past some more dubious stains and over several other black strings to the rap sheet of a rather uninteresting looking African American man, who's rap sheet was basically a road map of urban blight outlining why this country is in such desperate need of education reform. The second black string led further to the right, past a pair of shoulder holsters hung on a nail that had been pounded into the wall decades ago and on to the section of wall nearest the door of the room. Here, at the end of the string, was the rap sheet of a young guy, maybe twenty four. He was trying to look tough for the camera, but his eyes just screamed I'm going to get butt-raped tonight. His list of criminal activity was short: One arrest for purse snatching and another, just months later, for armed robbery. At the bottom of the page was that highlighted word again. Deceased.

Only one black string was coming out of the picture. It reached up to the ceiling and stretched across before coming down the opposite wall. Here, on the wall facing the butt rape scared young man was an older version of himself staring the eight feet across the room at him. Same last name. Father and son. Father had a much longer record. More of the old-school criminal type. Breaking and entering, burglary, armed robbery, et cetera. He had four strings coming out of his thumbtack. Three of them were black, one that same disturbing shade of red. He was also Deceased.

The red string continued halfway down the left wall of the room and was wrapped around the tack in a newspaper article about a residential burglary of some jewelry that had left no clues. The article was tacked to the wall right above an ancient single bed with no sheets and a mattress that looked as though someone had rescued it from a Civil War field hospital. From this article extended five more black strings, all leading to other rap sheets. Each of these had more black strings attached to them, some had the disturbing red, as well. The blacks all led along the walls to other crimes and rap sheets and eventually back to the map.

The red string crossed the wall over the bed and met up with four other red strings just above a beaten up old hot plate that was so covered with spilled food that it was hard to tell if the half eaten can of beans on top was a permanent fixture or just today's lunch which had melted down through the blackened leftovers of past meals to meet the actual surface of the plate itself. Each of the other red strings came from across the room in open space, not following the wall, where they started at another mug shot. From them more red strings stretched out into the room, spreading like poison ivy. Each of them ended in a mug shot with the highlighted word: Deceased.

Once the five red strings met on the wall, they wrapped around the corner of the room back onto to wall with the map. They were evenly spaced, marching in lock step like little columns of red-jacketed soldiers toward the city of Pittsburgh as portrayed by Rand McNally. Just before they reached the map, though, the five red strings came together, touching for the first time. They right-faced down the wall and ended dead center just below the map at a thumbtack which suspended a sheet of plain white paper just above a hard worn old writing desk. This paper had no notes about a crime, no image of a criminal, just a single word: Ash.

A cell phone on the desk vibrated. That rhythmic buzz, buzz. Buzz, buzz. Over and over again the phone danced on the table. The man sitting at the table ignored it and continued to make notes in a small black hardcover notebook. Spread out on the table were more police files and newspaper clippings, bundled together in two piles. The phone stopped buzzing.

The man opened another file. The phone began to rattle against the table again. The man continued to ignore it. He glanced through a file, and occasionally looked up at the map. Then he wrote down a date and address in his notebook with a short description. The phone stopped buzzing. The man rubbed his chin, the stubble making an audible scratching sound as his hand passed over his sharp jaw line and the hollow area between that jaw and his prominent cheekbones. The phone rattled on the table again. He glanced at it then rubbed his sunken, red eyes before going back to taking notes. The phone stopped vibrating.

The man stopped for a moment and moved his head from side to side, taking in the whole scene before him. He reached over and pulled a cigarette from one of the packs that littered the desk. He held it in his teeth while he dug in his pocket. Pulling a Zippo out, he flipped the lid open and flicked it into life. The phone began to vibrate again. The man shoved the lighter back in his pants and grabbed a bottle of whisky from the back corner of the desk. Untwisting the cap, he took a short swig before returning it to its place of honor, outside the clutter of the rest of the desk. He pushed the sleeves of his dress shirt up past his elbows and unplugged the phone from its charger before pressing the accept button. He put the phone to his ear.

"Hello?"

"Thomas? This is Father Daniel."

Tommy took a long drag from his cigarette, tapping ashes onto the floor. "Hello, Father. What can I do for you?"

"Well, I haven't heard from you in the four months since you left Baton Rouge, also I spoke to Michael, and he said he hadn't heard from you either." Tommy could hear Father Daniel's voice quiver, just a touch of it, but he could hear a nervous shaking in the old priest's breath.

"I've been busy, Father." Tommy put the phone on speaker and set it and the lit cigarette on the edge of the desk next to a loose pile of crushed out butts and a series of long, thin burns, the evidence of trying to smoke while maintaining a train of thought. He picked up his pen and jotted a couple of notes in his notebook.

"I understand that, Thomas. But I have been trying to call you for three months." Father Daniel took a drink of something. The sound of swallowing came through the phone loud and clear.

A moment later, Tommy heard the gentle clink of a china cup coming to rest on a saucer. Tea. It must be afternoon.

"Like I said, Father. I've been busy." Tommy picked up the cigarette and took a short drag before setting it back on the edge of the table.

"Well, I called to tell you that I talked to Michael. He is doing well despite what you put him through that night. He wanted you to know that he's back in classes." There was a harshness here, and indicting tone Tommy hadn't heard from Father Daniel before. That disapproving priest voice that is usually reserved for when you get someone else in trouble. Tommy, for the moment, chose to ignore it.

"That's good, Father." Tommy flipped through the stack of newspaper clippings, turning them over until he found the specific one he'd been looking for. He gave it a quick read before paper-clipping it to the mugshot next to his notebook in the center of the desk.

"Thomas, what happened down there? Everyone is looking for you. The Council of Cardinals have listed you as persona non grata. They say you attacked Brother Marcus and threatened the church leaders." Disbelief. After everything Father Daniel had found out about Tommy, after everything he'd been a part of covering up, Father Daniel still somehow couldn't believe that no one was safe from him. The priest thought Tommy had limits, that he had a respect for the church that would protect it. Father Daniel still thought there was a line Tommy wouldn't cross.

"I did all of that and more, Father. They're hiding something. They're hiding devices, and that's why they came after Father Paul's research." Tommy knew that what he'd done, what he was willing to do, was right. He knew how dangerous the devices the church built could be, and how dangerous keeping their existence a secret could become.

"You can't honestly think that the church is keeping a secret like that. Why would they?"

"Father, five hundred years ago the church built an army of devices to act as a Vatican guard. They lost control of them. Now, they claimed that the devices were destroyed, but the truth is, they lost them. These things are killing machines, and they're probably still out there somewhere, just waiting for someone to reactivate them. That's what Father Paul knew. That's what he was researching."

"How did you learn this?"

"When I questioned Brother Marcus, he told me everything. He tried to gloss it over, but he knows those things are still out there. He even went so far as to threaten me if I told anyone."

"That's not the story that Brother Marcus is telling, Thomas. He says that he was trying to help with your investigation and you attacked him while he was going through Father Paul's papers. He claims you are paranoid and erratic."

"I don't care what Marcus says. I did what I did for a reason, and he knows it. I'll settle up with him another time. Right now I have to finish up here." Tommy was frustrated. This back and forth with the old priest was wasting time, time he could be spending finding the link to Ash, the man whose cryptic message had brought him here. The man who was spreading devices all over the country. Maxwell Ash. Pinkerton, murderer for hire, immortal. Tommy's last chance, and last loose end. Father Daniel was distracting him from his goal. Was he doing it on purpose?

"Thomas, you can't settle up with him, not in the way I know you mean to. You have to stop. You've changed, son. I can hear it in your voice. You're obsessed with something. I don't know what, but it's tearing you apart. You have to stop killing and come home. Give all this up and try to live a normal life again. Where are you Thomas? You told Michael you were going to Pittsburgh.

Are you still there? Let me come get you. We can straighten all of this out." Father Daniel sounded scared, desperate. Was it fear for Tommy, or fear of something else?

"I can't tell you where I am, Father." Tommy had a bad feeling. This conversation had dragged on too long. Father Daniel was trying to get him to come in. Or was he just trying to keep Tommy on the phone so that someone could trace the signal?

"Why not, Thomas?"

"I tell you, and the church knows. Your loyalty is to the church, not the truth. I tell you, you tell the Jesuits, and they come for me just like they did with Father Paul." Tommy glanced out the grease streaked window. Was that truck there before?

"Thomas, you know me better than that. You're being paranoid. My loyalty is to you and all the other lost souls in this world. If you just tell me what you're doing, what you're looking for, and where you are, maybe I can help."

"You're not helping now, Father. I'll contact you when I'm done here."

"Thomas, please..."

Tommy pushed his finger into the end call button. He glanced out the window again. The truck was gone. Just up the block, a man sat on an overturned milk crate reading a newspaper. There was snow falling outside the window. It couldn't be more than twenty degrees out.

Tommy watched him for a few moments before pulling the SIM card out of the iPhone and slamming the phone into the edge of the table. Tommy's face twisted into a mask of blind rage. He let the phone fall to the floor and stomped on it until there was nothing left but a mangled case and glittery chunks of circuit board. Staring at the ruins of Katrina's phone, Tommy realized that he had just destroyed the app that let him track devices. That was the least of his concerns now, though. He was being watched, followed. He could feel it. He had to be more careful. You never know who you can trust.

Leaning back in his chair, Tommy rubbed his eyes again. He looked at the wall in front of him. The map was pockmarked with pinholes. Colored strings went everywhere, to the left, the right, up and over. Picking up the remainder of his cigarette, he relit it and took a final long drag off the butt before crushing it out on the corner of the table next to the now destroyed cell phone and pile of crushed out cigarettes.

The phone call from Father Daniel made him think about Buffalo. It was over a year ago now. He didn't like it, but sometimes he couldn't avoid it. He remembered Katrina Liu's face the first day she showed up at his office with a murder rap hanging over her head. Tommy liked to think that on that day, all of this started; that because of that one decision he was now in this shithole pay by week flophouse on the north side of Pittsburgh. He had tried to protect her, taken her into his safe house. He even got Father Daniel and Beaux involved in keeping her safe from the Khlysti, but none of it was enough.

Tommy looked up at the ceiling. That night at the forge. He tried to stop them then and there. He watched as they turned Dr. Katrina Liu, a noted physicist and possibly the most rational person Tommy had ever met, into little more than a puppet of Rasputin and his cult. He saw her smile at Rasputin's sidekick Vladmir Grozny. Tommy saw her turn on him. He heard the words when she told Grozny about Tommy's second pistol. He put a bullet in her neck.

He killed her. Tommy killed her. Not Grozny, not Rasputin, not one of their minions. Tommy did it. It was necessary. It was righteous. He didn't stop to think about it then, and he hadn't really thought about it since until now. Could he have saved her? At the time, he didn't think so. But the mind control couldn't have held forever. If it could, why would they need to keep broadcasting the signal? They wouldn't. There was a pretty good chance Tommy killed an innocent woman.

The worst part was, he didn't feel it. Still, even under the weight of that realization, he didn't feel anything. He wasn't bothered. There was no remorse. No feeling of guilt. He didn't have those emotions anymore. He knew that now. He felt nothing, really. Not even anger.

Tommy shook his head. There was a job to do. A man to find and finally put in the ground. Somehow, Maxwell Ash had survived and gotten ahold of devices. He was using them to try and overthrow governments, or at least to cause mayhem and hide his other illegal activities.

Glancing around the room, Tommy saw all the strings, all the interconnected spiderwebs of criminals and crimes. Most of these men were dead. Tommy didn't kill them. Someone was beating him to it, and taking them out so that they couldn't talk if they got caught. It was most likely Ash himself, or someone working for him. The devices they were using were disappearing, too. Tommy had to find the next link in the chain, find one of the men who hadn't been killed yet. He had to get ahead of the pattern, get to the next crime before the criminals.

Tommy closed his eyes. His mind's eye took in all the red strings. They glowed in his vision against the pallid squalor of the room. He scanned them. A connection. A link here, a crime there. Left to right across the room. Back and forth. From one deceased criminal to the next, following the trail.

Dates, times and locations spun around him as he followed a red string to a black one. It ended at deceased, but another red string branched off from there, leading to the burglary of a home in the mountains south of the city. One of the criminals attached to this string was still alive. Tommy could see the connection. He followed it. A jewelry store theft, stolen cars. He connected them all back to the same criminal. He wasn't dead yet. If he was, he hadn't been found. Another string led from him to a bank robbery. He followed other strings that connected to this man, to other criminals. More thefts. More bank robberies. Four men. Same pattern for all of them. Three were still alive.

Follow the patterns. Let the patterns lead the dance. Times and dates spun in his mind. A Thursday afternoon. A Friday night. A Tuesday. Three different crimes, three different criminals, three different days. No pattern. Have to go deeper.

He thought about the details of the case. Each place had been hit when it had the largest amount of whatever was stolen on hand. A jewelry store on Thursday afternoon, right after they got in a shipment of raw diamonds. A bar after closing but before the cash drop on Friday night, the busiest night of the week for them. A bank on Tuesday, the day that banks in the city get their deposit from the Federal Reserve. He glanced at a calendar on the desk. Today was Tuesday.

Tommy opened his eyes and stared at the map. He knew which of the red thumbtacks was each crime. There was a pattern here. Three wasn't many to develop a theory, but there was a pattern. He saw the banks. Five hit in the past two months on Tuesday. All hit with three man crews. Three living men on his walls. Now this was a pattern. Four of the banks hit at night. One in the late afternoon. Why was one different? Tommy closed his eyes again, went back through the files in his head. One of the pages had a coffee stain on it. Another, in a different folder, was double stapled. The bank that had been robbed in the afternoon was having maintenance done on their computer systems that night. There were supposed to be five or so people, not including security, in the building. That was why. The robbers knew there would be extra people in the bank that night, so they hit the bank earlier than originally planned.

But which bank would be next? Tommy looked at the five pins, mentally removing the rest of the markers that dotted the map. Where was the link? What made them the same? Why not hit the other banks in the city?

He stood up and glared at the map like it had insulted him, his nose just inches from the wall. Staring intently at one pin for several minutes before moving on to the next.

Ten minutes later, he was staring at the third pin when he let out a long, slow breath.

"Alleys." He muttered to himself. "They all have alleys."

Tommy dug through a small bag that was sitting on the floor next to the desk. He pulled out a cheap, international version of an Android phone and opened the case, sliding the iPhone's SIM card into the second SIM slot under the battery. He powered up the device and after choosing the new SIM, did a quick internet search of all the bank locations in downtown Pittsburgh. After filtering out all of the ATMs and other useless ads and not even remotely related shit that somehow gets tacked on to every internet search, he found the five that had been hit. A quick map search found the only other bank with an alley. It was a federal credit union at the corner of Grant Street and Strawberry Way, which itself was little more than an alley. If they held to the pattern, they'd hit that bank next. Most likely tonight.

Tommy pushed the chair out of his way and crossed the room. He found his least-wrinkled button down shirt and the jacket that matched his pants on the floor under the nail his holsters hung on. Sliding into the shirt, Tommy buttoned it up to his neck and tucked it firmly into his pants. He pulled a vest from another pile and pulled it on. It was a high button vest, and he buttoned it right to the top. After straightening his vest, he pulled his holsters off the nail and slid them over his shoulders. Lifting up the pillow on the stained, bare mattress, he pulled out his two Colt revolvers. They dropped into place in the leather holsters. He didn't intend to kill these men, well, at least not all three of them. At least, not yet. However, wounding them was an entirely different matter.

CHAPTER 2

Tommy parked his car on Fourth Avenue a few blocks from the bank. As he walked up Fourth, Tommy's eyes darted from side to side. He glanced at the rooftops as he crossed over Smithfield Street. There were way too many places for a sniper to hide in this city. For the first time in years, he felt that there was no anonymity in a city. He stood out, and he didn't know why.

The air stank of car exhaust. Even now, in the middle of winter with a cold wind blowing off the river, that smell stuck with him. Light flakes of snow drifted down from the darkening grey sky as he headed deeper into the city. It reminded him of when he walked these streets a hundred years ago. Back then, there were only a few cars here, owned mostly by the exceptionally wealthy. Pierce Arrows and Mercedes were the usual types they chose. A few of the socially mobile middle class had Model Ts, but there were still carriages clattering down these cobblestone streets.

Men still cleared the streets with shovels. A crew of three or four digging out a pathway wide enough for two carriages to pass. They didn't even remove the ice, just cleared out the deep snow where necessary to keep the carriages and new motorcars from getting stuck. Of course, this white snow that fell now was an anomaly. A century before, the snow was usually as black as the soot that poured from the smokestacks that surrounded the city on all sides..

Tommy stopped. The streets weren't cobblestone, not anymore. Not in a hundred years. He closed his eyes. He lowered his head, forcing the cobwebs out. A man passed him on the sidewalk. Tommy reached inside his overcoat and unbuttoned his jacket, preparing to reach for his guns, then stopped himself. The man kept walking, offering little more than a strange look at Tommy, this strange man who stopped in the middle of the sidewalk and reached into his jacket for no apparent reason. The man looked worn out. His hair, which had been slicked straight back on his head, had begun to fall forward as it got wetter in the falling snow. Several long strands fell over his face as he looked at Tommy. He was on the younger side, maybe mid twenties, with a heavy black overcoat buttoned all the way up to his neck and his collar turned up against the icy breeze. It was eight o'clock. The poor guy was probably was just walking back to his car after drinks with people from the office. He gave Tommy a final look and then turned the corner onto Smithfield.

Tommy glanced at the three rooftops again. The dark, looming forms of the buildings were a cold black silhouette against the grey, cloud filled city sky. The clouds swirled above his head as he walked up Fourth Avenue like the smog he remembered from so many years ago. He shook his head again. This was not smog. This was not nineteen twelve. Tommy turned the corner onto Grant Street.

It took Tommy about twenty minutes to make it to the building. Two hours later, he was still standing in the entranceway of the Allegheny Harvard-Yale-Princeton Club. Built in eighteen ninety, it was now a historic landmark. Tommy remembered it as a social club that was too exclusive for anyone but the most powerful in the city. Back then people of his social status, people who dressed in heavy work pants, rough shirts, and newsboy caps like him didn't walk by it with envy, they passed with hatred in their eyes.

Now dressed in a suit and tie, Tommy looked like just another member having a smoke outside.   People walking by just glanced and nodded at him, if they noticed him at all.   Luckily, this part of the entryway was unlit. Partially due to the building's location on what was more or less an alley, partially due to Tommy smashing out the lights that illuminated the building's courtyard.

From where he stood, he could see the whole back of the building which held the credit union. It was a modern skyscraper, all covered in marble and glass. When he last stood at this corner, there was a large brick building here, a dry goods warehouse or something similar. This whole area was closed off because the city was lowering the street level to remove the "hump" along Strawberry Lane. Now everything was flat and level. The only memory of that lost, chaotic city was the little alleyways that popped up between the huge modern buildings. Like most old cities, even the alleys had names. Nobody thought to do that anymore.

Even now, in the middle of this bustling modern city, Tommy could remember the hoof beats of the horse drawn cabs. They used to clatter down these narrow streets looking for fares. By this time of night, most of them were out of the downtown district, and had moved out to the areas where the theaters and restaurants were still buzzing.

That was before the war, before prohibition. Back then, the rich whooped it up at their dinner clubs and the poor hoped for at least one good meal before returning for another twelve hour shift at one of the many steel mills around the city. Hell, most of the people he'd known back then probably hadn't gone into downtown more than once a year unless they got called to a corporate office or were running an errand for one of their bosses.

Tommy watched the back of the building, trying to stay in the shadows. His vantage point only let him see down William Penn Place and along Strawberry Way. This gave him a clear view of pretty much the entirety of the back of the building. There were several large roll-up bay doors lined up at the back of the building, most likely for deliveries to the various offices and businesses that made up the huge skyscraper.

He was last here just before they started building the skyscrapers. Back then, the tallest building in downtown wasn't more than twenty stories. Now no self respecting developer would dare build anything smaller than that. All glass and steel. Something to be said for it, though. There was a glitzy, shallow beauty in it, but it lacked the permanence of brick and stone. Looking up at the glass and stone facade, those vertical rows of windows from top to bottom that made the whole place look like someone had painted black stripes on it, Tommy thought that it didn't look built to last. Nothing did anymore. Nothing was anymore.

Something drew Tommy's attention back to the base of the building. A strange orange-yellow glow seemed to emanate from the dark stone facade as though it was being superheated. As quickly as it formed, the glow faded leaving a film on the area that gave the appearance of a thin layer of clear ice over the stone. The section of stone that had been effected, near the corner opposite Tommy's position, started to undulate and roll as though it had turned to liquid. The polished granite rippled out from the center creating a ring of concentric waves about five feet across. It the dim light of the city's glow, it looked strangely like someone had dropped a pebble into a slate-grey pond.

A black duffle bag splashed through the effected section of wall, landing at the edge of the sidewalk. It was followed by two more. After the bags came through, the wall flopped back into position, the stone wobbling for a moment before settling back to a flat surface. So that was how they were getting in and out without being seen. Unless someone saw the beginning of the process or something moving through the wall, there was nothing to alert a passerby that anything was going on that was out of the ordinary. All they would see is a smooth stone wall if they even bothered to look.

A man dressed all in black with a ski mask over his face appeared through the wall next, followed by two more. The last man had a small wooden box in his hand. Tommy couldn't see it very clearly in the poor light, but the box looked like it had a winding lever on the side of it, like an old music box.

After the third man was through, he turned toward the wall and flipped a switch on the box. The ice-like effect seemed to melt away, disappearing first from the edges of the circle and moving quickly toward the center. In seconds it was gone completely, leaving no trace. Tommy slipped back into the darkness of the entranceway as the men picked up the duffle bags and, ran up William Penn Way, right past Tommy.

Tommy started after them when he noticed something on the roof of the building opposite the one that had just been robbed. Movement. A silhouette. Lithe, thin, smooth. Moving at almost superhuman speed along the rooftop, it was following the men on the ground. A lookout on the roof? Whoever it was, they were fast, navigating the edge of the building with sure footed confidence though Tommy knew from experience that in this cold the entire surface would be coated in a thin layer of ice that made even the act of walking treacherous. At that height, in these conditions of wind and freezing cold, running on the edge of rooftops was suicidal.

Tommy focused on the rooftop specter a split second too long, allowing the thieves to gain too much ground on him. He made a choice: Follow the lookout.

There were only a couple of cars parked on the street at this hour, and almost no traffic. Tommy sprinted down the center of the street staring up at the roof of the building and the shadow running along the ledge.

Before he knew it, he was in the intersection. Car horns blared as he bolted across Sixth Avenue to get a better look at the roofline. He heard tires screech, then felt the impact as he flipped over the hood of a sedan. His head hit something hard just before he went completely airborne. As he flew through the air over the car, he saw the thieves on the sidewalk less than a block up the avenue, stopped and staring at the accident.

He landed hard on his back and shoulder, rolling awkwardly into the gutter. He tried to get up, and his whole world spun. A man in a topcoat and tails climbed from his coach and asked if he was alright as Tommy dropped back onto the cobblestones.

Tommy shook his head, staring at the ground. The cobblestones went in and out of view, disappearing into the asphalt before floating back up through it. He gripped at the ground through

the dirty slush.   Asphalt.   Definitely asphalt.
Tommy looked up at the man standing over him,
he was dressed in a modern suit.   The carriage
melted into a late model sedan, it's windshield
smashed in by Tommy's head. He looked past the
man and saw the silhouette, standing stone still on
the rooftop like a gargoyle on a church. Looking
up the street, he saw the thieves duck into an
alleyway.   The shadow on the roof followed,
disappearing from view.

Dragging himself to his feet, Tommy picked
up his hat from the hood of the car and ran up the
street and into the alley. The men were already at
the other end, loading the duffle bags into a black
windowless van. His head was bleeding, he could
feel it. He looked up, wondering how the lookout
was going to get to the van from the top of the ten
story building.

He saw the shadow jump to the wall of the
building on the other side of the alley, gripping it
with hands and feet. It made another jump back to
the other side, descending about ten feet. After
four of these jumps, it landed on the ground about
twenty feet from Tommy.

He pulled his guns and shouted for whoever
it was to stop. The shadow didn't stop, it didn't run
for the truck. It ran at Tommy. Tommy cocked
his pistol and took aim. Before he could pull the
trigger, a sharp kick knocked the gun from his

hand. It clattered across the alley. Tommy blocked a right, then a left. Whoever this was, they were fast. Faster than Beaux, but not as strong.

Tommy managed to get a punch in that knocked his attacker back. He leveled his other pistol and fired for center mass. The shot echoed like thunder in the narrow alley. The shadow stopped momentarily, and Tommy finally saw its face, smooth, delicate features, large dark eyes. A long black ponytail draped over it's shoulder. A woman.

She didn't fall. She didn't even acknowledge the wound, instead she stepped forward and knocked the gun from Tommy's hand. Tommy prepared to block another punch, but instead she swept his legs. He landed hard on his back again, with her straddling him. He grabbed her throat, she grabbed his.

"Who are you working for?" She growled, pressing down on his windpipe with all her weight.

Tommy saw stars. "Where's Ash?" He growled back, pushing her up by her throat. His arm was just enough longer than hers to take the pressure off his neck.

"Who the fuck is Ash?" She said in a choked voice. Even though Tommy had a longer arm, she forced herself into his grip to try and regain her grip on his throat.

"The man you work for. The man behind the robberies. Where is he?" Tommy said, squeezing tighter.

The woman stared at him. Her eyes widened. "You don't work for the government?"

"No." Tommy said. "You don't work for Ash?"

"I don't even know who that is." She said loosening her grip slightly and shifting her weight back onto her knees.

Tires squealed at the end of the alleyway. The van took off in a cloud of burnt rubber and exhaust steam.

"Shit!" The woman exclaimed. She let go of Tommy's throat and bolted up the alley after the van.

Tommy tried to get up and chase her, but she was out of sight around the corner before he could struggle to his feet. He could hear sirens in the distance, a sure sign that either his meeting with the car or his gunshot, or both, had attracted the attention of the local police. He didn't have the time or the patience to try and explain what he was doing there.

Looking around the alley for a moment, he located his guns. He pushed back his overcoat and suit jacket and slid them into their holsters, buttoning his jacket and coat before making his way down to the other end of the alley and out onto the street.

As he walked back to his car, Tommy dabbed the blood from his head. There was a good bit of it. He had seen a lot of blood lately, too much of it had been his own. He pulled his phone from his pocket to check for messages. Nothing. He thought about the phone call from Father Daniel. He knew what persona non grata meant, but what did it really mean to him? He was out of the grace of the church. No more confession, no more absolution from sin. He couldn't take part in the sacraments. But he hadn't done any of that in years, anyway. The church must've known that. What were they trying to prove about his behavior?

In the past year he had maimed people, burned down buildings, and killed pretty much anybody who got in his way. But he was always in control. That was how he knew he was right. He never lost control. But then, there was Katrina's phone this afternoon, and the flashbacks.

Tommy made it to his car and got back to his room. He stripped his guns off and hung them on the nail near the door. Ducking under the strings he made his way to the desk and dropped his overcoat and jacket on the floor.

Lighting a cigarette, he pulled out his phone. He tapped the icon for his cloud drive and flipped through a couple menus. Soon he was staring at the scanned images of his research that Father Daniel had prepared for him. Good thing he thought to upload them to an anonymous cloud before he smashed the phone.

Tommy took several long drags of the cigarette as he thumbed through page after page. He hadn't taken the time to organize the information any better than it had been in his old library, so he prepared himself for a long search. He pulled another cigarette out of the pack and lit it off the smoldering butt of the first one, then crushed the first one out on the corner of the desk, leaving it still smoking and standing upright.

Five cigarettes and three glasses of whisky later, he still hadn't found the device. Tommy pulled a fresh pack of cigarettes from the carton on the floor next to the desk and stood up, making his way to the small cot. He tossed the unopened cigarette pack and the phone on the mattress and grabbed the can of cold beans from the hotplate. Digging around in the trash on the floor, he found a serviceable spoon and scooped a couple of mouthfuls between his thin, dry lips.

Dropping spoon and can back onto the hotplate, Tommy reached under the cot and pulled out a fresh whisky bottle. He twisted off the cap and took a deep swig, then clamped the cigarette between his teeth, picked up the phone, and flopped onto the cot.

Three hours, a bottle of whisky, two packs of cigarettes and one can of beans later, he found it. The device. Turns solid matter into liquid, allowing a man to pass through it. The designer, some Polish guy from the eighteenth century, thought it might have military applications. Tommy thought about his own brush with the Polish underground back in the forties. He silently wished he'd known about it then. They could've used it. The description went on. Apparently, this thing made its way around western Europe for over a hundred years. The last time any of the Watchmakers had seen it, or at least the last time it was mentioned, was on the Crimean Peninsula in eighteen fifty-three.

Crimean War. Rasputin was there. So was Adalai Merrick. Was it possible that Ash had found some stash of devices that Merrick had left behind? Or worse, was he getting them from Rasputin?

Tommy rolled onto his back. He hadn't caught him. He hadn't killed him. Rasputin was still out there, spreading his religious infection somewhere. He knew that eventually he'd have to catch up with Rasputin, though Tommy figured without a watchmaker, he was more or less harmless. Just another cult leader espousing another false salvation, like a televangelist or political pundit.

But Ash was getting these devices from somewhere. Either Rasputin was helping him, or he found them himself. The key here was Adalai Merrick.

Merrick had been a war hero. Tommy had studied him for years after he disappeared. The guy had been a spy in the Crimean War, held by the Russians for three years before he escaped. The Queen had a parade for him when he returned, made him a knight, for Christ's sake. Five years later, his wife died and Merrick disappeared with his daughter. There were rumors that his wife had been murdered, that foreign agents had done it to send a message. Merrick wouldn't say. He just disappeared into America, making a living as a maker of fine watches in Buffalo.

By the time Tommy met him, he was a twisted, ancient thing. Kept alive only by the devices he'd created. A slave of the very men who held him captive all those years ago, the same men who had threatened his family for generations. Merrick knew how dangerous the devices could be in the wrong hands. He gave his life to stop the wrong men from having them. Merrick wasn't the type of men to keep a stockpile of them where they could be found.

So that left Rasputin. The Mad Monk. A power hungry cult leader who seemed, like Tommy, to be immortal. He wanted to rule the world, to turn everyone to his own perverted version of faith, by force if necessary. He was there, in eighteen fifty-three. He was also there in eighteen ninety-eight. That night at the edge of the canal. He wanted Merrick's granddaughter, Eliza. Tommy could never figure out why, since Rasputin and the Khlysti already had Merrick and all the knowledge of the Watchmakers. Tommy tried to save her, and it cost him his mortality, very likely his soul, most certainly whatever he had left of his sanity at that point.

Of course, she did survive. But Tommy didn't know that until he met Merrick last fall. He had thought for a hundred years that everything he'd done had been in vain, that she'd drowned in that canal on the night the watch exploded and left Tommy trapped at 26 years old and as far as he knew, unable to die.

Rasputin stopped in time that night, too. It was his bullet, or that of one of his men, that destroyed the watch.

So Rasputin it was. Tommy hadn't heard anything about him in months. There hadn't been any strange activity that he could've easily attributed to Rasputin or his cult. Maybe this was because he was using Ash now, who somehow survived over a century all on his own.

CHAPTER 3

The next morning Tommy made his way back through the windy winter streets to the credit union. The scene had changed since last night. There were people everywhere. Businessmen wandered about in their suits and ties, their expensive pants being ruined by the combination of mud, salt, and snow that collected in the gutters this time of year.

Women in skirts and jackets and sneakers, their more business-like heels held in one hand, did their best to jump over the puddles and avoid the slicker parts of the sidewalks. Sometimes they had the aid of male or female friends, sometimes they just fell down.

Tommy made his way to the doors of the building. There were cops everywhere, and Tommy's paranoia was screaming in the back of his head like a two-year-old throwing a tantrum on an airplane. As he walked through the front entrance, he saw even more cops in the lobby. He could see the credit union from where he stood, but there was a gauntlet of about thirty cops, a mixture of plainclothes detectives and uniformed officers, blocking his way.

He got about three quarters of the way through before a small, thin, and apparently very young uniform stepped in front of him.

"Where do you think you're going, buddy?" The cop asked, smacking his gum between every word.

"My name is John Smith, I have to make a deposit." Tommy was thinking on his feet. This cop took his job more seriously than most. Young cops normally do, they haven't seen enough to dull their sense of honor and that strange, bullying privilege that police seem to feel yet. Tommy tried to step around him.

"No, you're not. The bank is closed." The cop said, sidestepping to stay in front of Tommy.

"What happened in there?" Tommy said.

"Place got robbed last night. We're still looking into it." The cop responded. He was full of shit. He wasn't looking into anything. He was standing it the lobby, stopping curious onlookers from getting too close to where the real investigators were working. At best, he was a security guard.

"But, I have to make a deposit..." Tommy tried to make his voice sound pleading, like his wife would kill him if he didn't get this done. It wasn't an easy trick for him to pull off. Right now, he just wanted to snap this little twit's neck.

"There's another branch down off Sixth. About five blocks from here. Go do it there. There's no tellers in here, anyway." The cop gestured over his shoulder, indicating the direction of the other branch.

"Do they know who did it?" Tommy asked.

The cop adjusted the front of his gun belt and left out a long sigh between snaps of his gum. "We can't discuss an ongoing investigation. Now please, move along, sir."

This guy might as well have been a rent-a-cop. He didn't actually know shit. Not uncommon. Most of the time, the beat cops never had any idea what was going on in an investigation unless they interviewed witnesses or actually caught the suspect. All the real work was done by the detectives.

"Okay. Thank you, officer." Tommy said. He turned and started to walk out. As he crossed the lobby, a group of about nine crime scene investigators in their white disposable suits and carrying heavy tool cases were walking in, flanked by two uniforms who were wearing jackets that said Forensics on the left chest.

One of the uniforms caught Tommy's eye. It was a little tighter than it should have been. It was tailored to fit a woman's body. He looked up at the face. Large eyes, green with dark eye shadow and liner. A long black ponytail hanging down under her hat. Smooth, delicate features. The woman from the alley.

She caught Tommy's eye as they passed. She let a slight, crooked smile flash across her face as they glanced at each other. Then it was back to business. The same cop who had stopped him stepped in front of her, but with a couple of quick, harsh words about chains of evidence and biological degradation, the young patrolman cowered and the whole group was allowed to pass into the crime scene.

Tommy continued out the door, trying to figure this out. Was she a cop? Was that a disguise? People like that don't really exist. He had been alive for a hundred and forty two years, and never once had he even heard of a vigilante who runs around rooftops at night, only to return to their day job as a cop, completely unnoticed. This wasn't a comic book. There are no superheroes. For that matter, there weren't really any heroes at all.

He passed through the revolving glass doors of the building onto the covered section of the sidewalk. The marble and glass front face of the building hung over his head, supported by piers sheathed in stainless steel and yet more marble. A solid, heavy, brutish symbol of dominance. Like medieval cathedrals, high-rises were designed to remind you of who was really in charge. Years ago, it was the steel men. The titans of industry that built the country on the backs and sweat of poorly paid and even more poorly treated workers, most of them immigrants. Now, in modern Pittsburgh, it was the bankers.

Tommy looked around. The crowd had gotten thicker since he went inside. That was no surprise. People see police cars and crime scene tape and want to know what happened. It was human nature. Kind of a silent way of knowing that your day isn't really going that bad, even if your breakfast was burned. It was also grotesque. People stared at dead bodies under tarps like they were looking at freaks from a sideshow. They stared, wondering who was under there, making up stories in their minds about the dead body's family, the wife and child crying at home. Or they thought about how evil that dead person must have been, taken out in an act of righteous fury by some jilted lover or rival drug dealer of gang member. Otherwise perfectly normal people could stare at a tarp with a body under it for hours, getting a sick thrill from it, knowing that they would have a story to tell their friends over beers that night. Perfectly normal people could stare at the tarp, but God forbid you ever remove it and show them what was underneath.

There were people milling around everywhere. It was nearly nine o'clock. Start of the business day. Most of the people gave a cursory glance at the crime scene tape and ignored it, figuring it would be on the news. A lot were on their cell phones, wrapped up in heavy coats and hats and scarves and gloves against the cold, biting air that whipped through the artificial caverns of a high rise city at nearly hurricane force. They were just trying to get into their warm offices before the boss noticed that they were running late. You could tell which ones were the bosses. They didn't seem to be in any hurry. Tommy turned his own collar up against the wind.

Tommy started up the block. It was four blocks to the lot where he had parked. If he made it there before nine he could get out without having to pay the daily rate to the attendant, a man who, even at eight a.m., stank of unwashed clothes, pot and booze. Tommy figured by the look of the guy, he hadn't seen a sober day in twenty years.

As Tommy got close to the end of the block, a man in a dark suit standing on the opposite corner caught his eye. He looked to be in his mid-thirties, but he had an air of authority that made it entirely possible was he was considerably older. The man was slightly above average height, and thin, almost rakishly so. His charcoal grey suit was a tailored English style, cut close to the body and single breasted. Tommy guessed Savile Row. He spoke into his phone intently, deftly dodging the throngs of people moving in every direction around him. He seemed to be paying no attention to anything but his phone. Tommy knew this was an act. The man kept sneaking glances at him. Also. Why was this idiot not wearing a coat in twenty degree weather? Even if he had just come down from his office to have a smoke, he would have put his coat on.

His shoes were the kicker, though. Nothing on them. Clean, dry. Nice as the day he'd had them made. This guy wasn't a worker, not around here. He had gotten out of a car in downtown, and recently. He didn't get out to make his call, either. He got out to watch Tommy.

Tommy turned around at the corner, making an expression he hoped would convey that he had forgotten something. Everyone seemed to be glancing at him as he turned. Men in suits and ladies in that modern uniform of the white collar woman, the skirt suit, watched as they passed by. He swore he saw one man take his picture with a camera phone. He looked across the street. There was a youngish man with slicked-back hair. Tommy had seen him before. He *knew* he had. Something about the upturn of the collar of his overcoat. That young, tired face. Jesus, everyone was watching him, following him.

He heard a car stop at the curb behind him. Something big, heavy. Not limo heavy, but at least a Town Car. Two men in dark suits were standing talking under the awning of the Kopers Building. One was on his phone. As Tommy passed them, the man closed his phone and stepped in front of Tommy.

"Mr. McKinney?" The man asked. He wasn't large, maybe Tommy's size under the coat and bulletproof vest that he was trying to hide under his dress shirt.

"Sorry, you've got the wrong guy." Tommy did his best Pittsburgh accent and tried to step past. The second man blocked his way.

Man number two leaned in close. "Mr. McKinney, we know who you are. You're to come with us." The man reached inside Tommy's coat and pulled out his Peacemakers, holding them close between the two of them to keep them out of sight.

The first man leaned in. "We don't want a fuss." He said. He had an accent. European, maybe German?

These guys didn't want attention. They didn't want a show. There were forty cops sitting less than a block away. All Tommy had to do was scream or fight. Before he could act on it, there was a gun in his back. The first guy had stepped in behind him, pressing the barrel of a semi-automatic against his spine. Tommy could feel the snub of the barrel, the sharp edge of the slide pressing into his flesh.

Tommy heard the big car again. The men ushered him to it, still pressing the gun into his lower back. The second man opened the door and walked around to the other side. Once in the car, the men sat on either side of him. The car pulled away from the curb and drove for a few blocks and pulled into an alley.

"We're going to need you to put this on." The second man said, holding a black hood in front of Tommy.

"Come on, guys. I promise I'm not going to tell anyone where your boss's secret lair is. That thing's going to mess up my hat. Besides, it'll clash with my suit." Tommy said, looking from one thug to the other.

The first man grabbed Tommy's hat and tossed it on the front passenger seat.

"Okay, fine." Tommy said. He grabbed the heavy black hood and slid it over his head. He didn't think these guys wanted to kill him. If they did, they could do it right here, in the alley. There was a lot of traffic noise, and guys like this generally had access to silencers.

They drove for what seemed like miles. The car was nearly silent, except for the driver's turn signals. He seemed to be turning a lot. It gave Tommy the impression that they hadn't left downtown.

After maybe an hour of driving, they went downhill. Tommy could hear the sound of an underground parking lot. That odd, echoing sound of engines and car doors and tires squeaking on polished concrete in a concrete cave.

"A parking garage?" Tommy said. "Are you guys really that stereotypical? I mean, come on. This isn't nineteen seventy. You might as well have taken me to an island with a hollowed out volcano." Tommy heard a muffled snort from the driver. The man to his right made a sound, then the car was silent again.

Moments later, the car came to a stop. Tommy had no idea how far underground he was, but he could feel from the damp, warm air that it was at least a story. The men on either side of him got out of the car. They pulled Tommy out. The car pulled away. Tommy stood with the hood still on. They must have known this garage will be empty, or they owned the building. He knew from experience that holding a man in a hood in a place where just anyone could walk in could be disastrous for a kidnapping.

One of the men took him by the elbow and led him across the open space of the parking structure. The sound of keys. An elevator bell. Someone pushes Tommy forward. More keys. Then something that sounded like numbers being pressed into a keypad. The elevator doors slid shut.

The elevator wasn't standard. He didn't need to be able to see it to know that. It smelled sanitized, heavily. Industrial cleanser that had been thoroughly rinsed and a scented air sanitizer of some kind. This wasn't a service elevator, though. Not meant for workmen. The floor squeaked under their shoes. It was polished, possibly marble.

A fancy elevator which takes both keys and a key code to get it moving? This was a very, very secure building. Where they didn't want stains in the elevator. CIA, maybe. Not FBI. They were too public to have secret elevators and take people off the street without warrants. Even the CIA wasn't big on doing it on US soil. They weren't actually allowed to work domestically. So who was dragging him up a secure elevator in an undisclosed location?

Tommy heard the familiar ding of the elevator bell followed by the sound of the doors sliding open. He was again taken by the elbow and led out into what he assumed was a hallway. He could hear phones ringing and being answered. Men and women speaking quietly as he passed. Obviously an office of some kind. The men led him straight for a while, then the path twisted and turned several times, to the point that Tommy figured they must have doubled back on themselves. Finally, they two agents stopped. He heard a key card swiped, then the sound of a lock bolt retracting. A doorknob turned, and the door opened. An arm shoved Tommy into a room.

He could feel the buzz of electronic equipment in the air. It was making the hair on his arms stand up a bit. He could hear the small cooling fans of computers through the hum, buzzing along dutifully. One of the agents led him to a chair and sat him down. He felt them untying the bag over his head.

As the sack was pulled off, Tommy expected to be blinded. Instead, he was greeted by the dim, blue glow of computer screens in an almost black room. There was a bank of monitors five wide and four high opposite his chair, about fifteen feet away. Each monitor showed something different. Some were just lines of data, running in a continuous stream, ever upward. Others were traffic cameras, security feeds, closed circuit television systems with data overlayed on the images. Height, weight, criminal records appearing as the cameras focused on one individual at a time. Facial recognition was running at amazing speed on one of the screens, flashing data about the people who were being picked up on the other monitors. Birth dates, addresses, personal habits, employment information, criminal records. One screen showed only Tommy's face, the program was measuring the distance between his eyes, the length of his nose, the angle of his jaw. Huge chunks of data appeared and disappeared around his image, giving different names, dates of birth, addresses, DMV records, police records, photographs. Whoever this was, it seemed they were tapped into every single source of information available, and they were doing their homework.

A man stepped out of the shadow to the side of the bank of monitors. He was tall and thin, dressed in an immaculate dark suit. The man from the sidewalk earlier. The man who had been watching him as he left the bank. The man stepped in front of the monitors, making himself a partial silhouette.

"Hello, my name is Mr. Brinson. Do you know where you are, Mr. McKinney?" The man said, a touch of accent in his voice.

Tommy tried to focus on the voice. He knew the accent, but it was so slight, he couldn't place it. "My guess would be in a high rise. Somewhere in Pittsburgh judging by the turns your driver took. We never left downtown."

Tommy saw just a hint of a smile in the gloom.

"That's true. But do you know what this room is? Where we've brought you?" The man had an ease about him that put Tommy off. He had his hands in his pockets, and was leaning up against the desk.

Tommy shook his head.

"You're in a very special place, Mr. McKinney. That much I'm sure you've already figured out. From here," the man gestured to the desk and bank of monitors behind him, "I can monitor everything that goes on in Pittsburgh and beyond. The movement of any individual, the conversations of any group. I can detail the patterns of a person's life and then extrapolate what they're going to do next."

"Isn't that sweet? So the government *is* monitoring our every move. Honestly, I don't give a shit. If you were going to kill me, you would have by now, and you don't seem like the arresting type. Why am I here?" Tommy leaned back in his chair.

"You're here, Mr. McKinney, because of your actions last night and this morning. And, of course, who you choose to associate with." The tall man turned around and typed something on a keyboard.

The screens went blank, then one image appeared, taking up all the screens. It was Tommy last night, fighting with the woman in the alley. The man then clicked the mouse again and a still image from this morning appeared of the woman and Tommy passing in the bank.

"I would ask you what you were doing in that alley chasing bank robbers last night, but I know you'll never give me a straight answer, and quite frankly, I don't really care. What I do want to know it this: Do you know who this woman is?" The man pointed at the woman in the picture.

"Never saw her before last night. I have no idea what she was doing there. I figured she was with the bank robbers. Why do you want to know?"

"We already know. We want you to know who you're dealing with, Mr. McKinney." The man picked up a folder from the desk and started reading.

"Known alias: Allison. Real name: Redacted. Former Army explosive ordinance expert, captured by insurgents in Afghanistan, two thousand eight. Escaped from mental health unit of Walter Reed Army Medical Center two thousand ten after killing a fellow patient and an orderly. At that point she disappeared. We assume that she was turned during her captivity in Afghanistan. In twenty-eleven, she reappeared, now acting as a single-person cell for unknown terrorist organization. Possibly for-hire mercenary. Strong anti-American sentiment. According to her medical records," the man flipped a couple of pages "Patient shows no fear of pain or punishment and a strong desire to cause harm to others. Possibly psychopathic. Refuses to respond to questions in a direct manner. Has shown willingness to use sexuality to gain control of situations. Insists on a minimum of five hours of strenuous physical activity per day. Patient shows hyper-vigilance usually associated with Post Traumatic Stress Disorder, coupled with heightened sensory recognition and reflexes, most likely due to her high level of physical fitness. Multiple types of mood-altering and sedative medications administered. None seemed to have any effect, even in dangerously high doses. Patient should be regarded as extremely dangerous and, unless extraordinary improvement is achieved, should be remanded to the highest level of security."

Tommy tried not to smile. She sounded like his kind of lady.

The man set the folder back on the desk. "That was written the day she broke out. The day she killed a patient by pushing her finger through his eye socket and into his brain. The orderly's death I'll spare you the details of."

"Oh, don't spare the details. I'm beginning to like her." Tommy smiled, leaning forward in his chair.

The man walked closer, giving Tommy a clearer view of his high, sharp cheekbones and angular face. He leaned in. "She ripped his dick off and shoved it down his throat. He suffocated on it."

Tommy shifted back in his chair. "Well, that certainly begs a question."

"What's that, Mr. McKinney?"

"What was he doing with his dick out?" Tommy smiled. He knew exactly what the orderly was doing. Same thing asylum workers had been doing to female inmates for centuries. "Sounds to me like he deserved it." He said.

The man straightened up. He knew what had happened in that hospital, too. "She killed two people, then started making plans for an attack on the government. Not to mention at least thirty unconnected murders since then that we *know of* and God knows how many other crimes. She is well-funded, well armed, well trained, and an enemy of the state."

"What do you want me to do about it?" Tommy finally recognized the accent. Scottish, but he'd tried hard to lose it.

"We don't want you to do anything, unless you see her again. If you do, you put a bullet in her. If you can do that, then we are willing to forgive your past... Indiscretions." The man walked back to the desk and picked up another folder, dropping it in Tommy's lap.

Tommy flipped through the file. It had detailed descriptions of everything that had happened in the past year, from the day Katrina Liu walked into his office to last night and his run-in with the hood of the car. Photographs, news clippings, ballistics reports, Tommy's burned aliases, everything. There was enough information in this file to lock Tommy in a tiny little cell on a tiny little naval base on a tiny little Communist island in the Caribbean for eternity. Something told Tommy this guy wouldn't even flinch at the idea.

"Who are you, Brinson?" Tommy said, still staring at his file.

"We're the kind of people you don't screw with, Thomas James McKinney, date of birth, *unknown*. You find Allison. You kill her. That file disappears."

The hood was pulled over Tommy's head again and he was led back out of the room.

CHAPTER 4

It was dark when they pulled the hood off Tommy. The thugs in the car had driven him around for several more hours before stopping again right where they had picked him up. One of the men slid Tommy's pistols back into their holsters and pushed Tommy's hat back onto his head before shoving him out of the black sedan. The car sped away from the curb and disappeared around the corner.

Tommy adjusted his jacket and started down the street toward his car. He would definitely have to pay the full day rate now, if his Jag hadn't been towed. He could smell that strange end of day scent in the air, like a mixture of stale exhaust fumes and desperation. He tried to keep his eyes to the ground, looking for those slick spots that always seemed to form in the most random places. Also, he had a new fear of the cameras that seemed to be everywhere. It wasn't just a matter of thinking people were watching him now. He knew it was a fact. There was a force in this city that was watching not just him, but everyone. Every cell phone call, every ATM transaction, every choice whether to turn left or right at an intersection was being scrutinized for patterns, or breaking patterns.

He had travelled maybe five blocks and was passing an alley when he heard a quiet voice come from the darkness.

"Hey, you." It said, in a subtle, feminine tone. Not aggressive, but confident, almost coquettish.

Tommy turned and peered into the black darkness of the midwinter night. A shape formed from the shadows. Leaning up against a wall, one leg propped up on the bricks. Arms crossed over the chest in a pose familiar to any man who had ever kept a woman waiting.

"I've been waiting for three hours." She said, pushing herself off the wall.

Tommy reached into his coat, but she put her hands out, showing she was unarmed. Tommy knew better. Even without a gun, at a distance of less than ten feet, this woman was dangerous. Beyond that, she was dangerous company. Tommy scanned the buildings for security cameras.

"There aren't any." She said, reading his eyes. "That's why I picked this spot."

His quick scan told him she was right. "I'm supposed to kill you, you know." Tommy said.

"I know. You've been talking to Brinson. I saw them take you off the street." She kept herself in the relative shadows of the alleyway, leaving Tommy looking like a madman talking to an empty alley to anyone who passed by. "There's a lot he didn't tell you, though. There's something going on, and I think you need to know about it. Follow me." She backed into the blackness. Tommy followed her into the darkness of the alley, having no idea what to expect.

Once in the alley and out of the glare of the streetlights, Tommy could see more clearly. The woman Brinson had called Allison was dressed in a black fitted turtleneck and skin tight pants, or leggings, he couldn't tell. She was wearing black leather knee-high boots with a smooth sole. In the dim light of the alleyway, she looked to Tommy's eyes to be made of black fabric and menace.

There was a black, late model SUV parked part way down the alley, taking up pretty much the whole width. It wasn't the van he had seen at the robbery the night before. Was it possible that she was tracking them, just like he had been?

She slid between the wall of the alley and the side of the gleaming black truck. As she got to the driver's door, she motioned Tommy to go to the passenger side. Tommy did so. If she had wanted to kill him, she could have done it last night, or moments ago when he was passing the alley. She had other plans. His gut said she was being honest, and there was more to this than met the eye. From his experience, there always was.

Tommy slid into the passenger seat and pulled the door shut. Glancing into the back of the truck, he saw military style reinforced plastic shipping cases, four of them, laid out in the back behind the seats.

"Put your seatbelt on," Allison said, "you're going to need it." She started the engine and threw the truck into gear, flying out into the street without checking the traffic. Horns blew as the truck tires squealed on the pavement. The truck momentarily jostled from side to side before settling down and roaring down the street. She threw the truck around two more corners before slowing to legal speeds and obeying the traffic laws.

"If the cameras don't catch you within the first few blocks, odds are that they won't be able to pick you out of the traffic." She said, looking at Tommy's hand clenched on the door handle.

Tommy noticed that she was taking main, heavily trafficked streets and staying off the less used side roads. It was part of the overall plan, he figured, to get the truck lost in traffic. The vehicular equivalent of disappearing into a crowd.

They travelled around the city for close to an hour, sometimes headed north, sometimes south. A few times they clearly doubled back on their own trail. Tommy knew this trick, too. If anyone was following in a car, there were better odds that you could see them by doubling back like this, forcing them to pass you repeatedly to try and stay hidden. It had the secondary advantage that if you were being followed, you could get away from your tail without them really knowing what direction you were ultimately headed. Or, as Tommy figured was the case with Allison, get behind them so that you could get the drop and ambush them, instead of being caught in an ambush yourself.

They drove on for what seemed like an eternity. Tommy watched Allison's face as they drove. Her lips turned upward at the corners in just a slight hint of a smile. Her body gave no indication of the underlying physical strength. Her thin arms looked like they'd have trouble opening a stuck jar lid, much less throwing a right hook that could make a grown man see stars.

He wondered how she could move so well in such tight clothes. Being this close to her, he could see that what he thought was leggings was actually black denim, stretched tightly over smooth, muscular legs. There was something under her fitted turtleneck that he couldn't quite make out, something pressing against the fabric from the inside.

She glanced at him out of the corner of her eye, catching him looking her over. Her bright red smile got a little bigger.

"See something you like?" She said, turning her eyes back to the road.

"Not in particular." Tommy said, turning his face back to the passenger side window.

Those full, red lips pouted. "Aww. You keep that up, you're gonna hurt my feelings." She said in a strange sort of mocking tone.

"If I got turned on by every dangerous woman I've met, I'd never get anything done." Tommy said, still looking out the window.

"So you think I'm dangerous?"

Tommy thought about the look in her eyes last night, the dilated pupils, the smile on her face as she tried to choke the life out of him. "Lady, I know you're dangerous."

"Then why did you get in the truck?"

"Like I said; if I didn't associate with dangerous people, I'd never get anything done." Tommy said.

Allison smirked. She turned the wheel and swung the truck to the right into the yard of what looked like an abandoned warehouse. The truck bounced through the rutted and pot holed ground as she maneuvered around the back of the building. She pushed a button on the dash and a roll-up garage door in the wall groaned into motion, slowly for the first foot, then faster and faster until its full length was tucked neatly away against the ceiling. The whole process had taken less than ten seconds.

Pulling in through the hole left by the open door, Allison brought the truck to a stop. She pushed the button on the dash again and the door fell back down, slamming against the floor with a violent thud. She cut the engine and hopped out of the truck. Walking over to a bank of switches, she flipped them on. As the lamps on the ceiling heated up, the room was bathed in the yellow-green glow of mercury vapor light.

As Tommy climbed from the passenger seat, the room around him faded into being. What looked at first like a huge, black, gaping chasm was actually a mixture of living and training space. To his left there was a strange collection of tubes and ropes suspended from the ceiling in a rough approximation of a military agility course, but much, much more complex. The highest point, Tommy estimated, was close to forty feet from the floor. There was nowhere to hook a safety harness.

Off to the right was a small cot and an area for cooking, and another area separated from everything else by a set of wire-grate walls from which hung guns, ropes, climbing gear, batons, all sorts of equipment, most of which looked military grade or better. Through the metal grating Tommy could see a desk and a work table. On the desk, a computer was waking up.

Allison headed toward the small sleeping and eating space and Tommy followed. As she walked through a small gap in the temporary walls, she pulled off her turtleneck revealing what looked like for all intents and purposes a black corset covered in scales. As she turned her back Tommy could see that it was held in place with five Velcro straps, the same basic design as a modern bulletproof vest, but perfectly tailored to her form. She turned her head and again caught him looking.

"Dragon skin," She said, letting out a sigh as she released the Velcro closures. "stronger than kevlar, and more flexible. It's experimental. I *liberated* a sample from a military testing site and made this. Take a look, that forty-four round you tagged me with last night barely left a dent."

She turned to face him and pulled the corset off. Tommy averted his eyes, more out of habit than concern for her dignity.

"Oh," She said, passing the corset to him and revealing a black tank top underneath. "don't worry, I never give anything away for free." She leaned in close to him, way closer than was comfortable, considering that she'd nearly killed him with her bare hands less than twenty-four hours ago. Looking up into his eyes, she smiled again, a dark, seductive smile.

As quickly as she'd stepped into his space, she was out of it again. She turned and walked toward the small eating and sleeping area and pointed to a chair. "Have a seat." She said. As she walked away, Tommy watched her.

He was trying to put the pieces of this together. Who was this Allison? She wasn't just a terrorist, he could see that by the fact that this Agent Brinson and whoever he worked for had gone outside their agency to try to kill her. That wasn't something that any government agency does lightly, too much chance of a fuck-up making headlines. Beyond that, there was something strange about her, something he couldn't put his finger on. She had a warm, sultry smile, and she knew it. She had a sexy sway in her walk, and she knew it. She had nothing but death in her eyes. She knew that, too. So who was she? Tommy looked at the custom made corset in his hands as he sat in the chair. Right in the center of the chest one of the overlapping scales had a forty-four sized dent in it. Must've hurt like hell, but it hadn't even slowed her down.

Looking to his right, Tommy saw a police uniform hanging from the metal grating between an M16 and a semi-automatic shotgun. It was freshly pressed and clean, sheathed in a clear plastic bag from a dry cleaner.

"The police generally have no idea what they're looking for," Allison said, reappearing from the living area with her hair pulled back in a loose ponytail. "I do."

"Do you?" Tommy asked.

Allison walked over to the desk and typed on the laptop for a moment. "Yes, I do. Come here and look." She said, gesturing to the computer.

Tommy rolled his chair over to the desk. What he saw on the screen astounded him. There were pages, and folders of pages, of classified documents. There was too much for his eyes to take in in one shot, but it looked like Allison had somehow gotten ahold of everything the government had on watchmakers and devices. Some of the things he was seeing went back to World War Two and further. He didn't have time to read all of it, but he could see that his name came up a lot. It looked like the folder that Agent Brinson had given him was just the tip of the iceberg of what the government actually knew about him and his activities over the past hundred years, but most of their documentation stopped around nineteen forty five, except for one file that had the information about the Khlysti in Buffalo and everything he'd done since. Christ, why did he have to get involved?

"They've been using some Russian cult to spread fear, to keep control." Allison said, interrupting his train of thought.

"The Khlysti." Tommy said, still reading the screen.

"Yeah, that's them. The government has some kind of deal with their leader where he gives them access to these devices that you've been hunting for and in return, they let him do pretty much whatever he wants. Both ends work for them, because cults scare people into relying on the government to protect them, and they get access to these devices to do research and testing."

"Research and testing? What kind of research and testing? Are they trying to weaponize the devices?"

Allison chuckled. "If only it was that simple. Here, look." She moved the mouse and opened another file.

Inside there were digitized copies of files from the early nineteen nineties. Photographs, some digitized video, and pages and pages of documents, all about young children under the age of five.

"From what I've been able to find out, in nineteen forty eight Eisenhower authorized the agency that we now call DARPA to start testing devices on military personnel. The Russians had begun a similar project, and it started an arms race to create super soldiers with devices."

"So why are all of these files about children? None of them could have been soldiers."

"From what I've read, by the late eighties it was pretty clear that the negative effects of the radiation these devices put out far outweighed any benefit a soldier could gain from exposure."

"If you're not immune to it, like some people are. I've seen what the negative side effects do to you. It's not pretty."

"No, it's not." She said. "I've seen enough video of it to know that it's a horrible way to die."

"If you're lucky enough to die." Tommy said, rubbing the scar on his hand.

"Exactly. Anyway, they figured out that it wasn't working on adults, but they thought that if they managed to get in early enough, to focus the effects of the devices on a *developing* mind and body, then they might be able to mitigate the side effects as the child grew."

"They tested the devices on *children?*" Tommy said. His eyes widened as she flipped through photograph after photograph of children being exposed to devices. Some were clearly under a year old.

"They got their best results with infants. For some reason, if they managed to get ahold of them before they turned one, their minds and bodies were less likely to have negative effects from the radiation."

"Well, that makes sense, a baby's body can heal wounds much faster than an adult or even an older child can; that's why they don't scar as easily."

"Regardless, they still found that the negative effects were too great. A hundred kids were in the original test group, only forty four survived the testing. Of those, zero percent managed to survive it without some form of either mental or physical illness. Most of them so severe that they're probably spending their lives in institutions."

"Probably? Where did they get the kids from that they don't know where they ended up?"

"They set up fake families and adopted orphans. The whole thing was run by a secret branch of DARPA and funded by the CIA and NSA. After they shut the program down, the whole paper trail having to do with the children's identities was permanently redacted except for their letter designations from the testing program. It's all gone, no trace left anywhere."

Tommy turned to face Allison. "What does this have to do with Maxwell Ash? That's who I'm here for."

"I've never seen any mention of anyone by that name. I don't know who he is, but he's not involved with the government or the Khlysti. From what I've seen, they keep pretty tight surveillance on anyone who has devices."

"This guy has been at it as long as I have. Is there a chance he's in there under an alias?"

"They've got all of your aliases in here. Something tells me that they keep an even closer eye on..." She leaned in next to his ear and whispered. "People like you."

"So where do you come in to this?" Tommy said, turning to face her. Their faces were just inches apart, but Tommy's rage at her knowing his history blocked any attraction he might have felt. All he felt was a cold, hard anger.

Allison stepped back, breaking eye contact. "After they realized that children didn't work, they decided to try soldiers again." She walked over to the work bench and began fiddling with a pistol, pulling it apart and cleaning it. "The theory was that we had much better psychological training and that because of the treatments we were given to combat radioactive and biological attacks that we might be less likely to develop radiation psychosis or physical side effects."

"Brinson told me you were a soldier."

"Yeah, Afghanistan." She said, still cleaning the pistol. "Eighty First Airborne. I was an explosive ordinance specialist, a bomb diffuser."

"What happened?" Tommy said, turning his chair to face the workbench.

"It was September, two thousand eight. We were on patrol ahead of a convoy. There were four Humvees in my unit, sixteen of us in all. Our mission was to clear the road of possible IEDs before the convoy came through. They had some kind of VIP with them or something. Anyway, we were checking a section of the Kabul-Garden Highway headed south toward Garden. There was a good chance that we'd get ambushed, the war was still pretty hot then. We were on high alert. Anyway, about four miles outside Garden we hit this little village, no more than a few huts. Ever seen a place like that?"

"I was raised in a place like that."

"Huh." She said, placing the pistol on a hook attached to the metal grating behind the workbench. She pulled down an MP5, began to field strip it, and continued her story. "So we come into this little village, and it's quiet, like, really quiet. Back then, that wasn't that strange. There had been a lot of fighting in the area, and a lot of the locals had taken refuge in the larger cities. The place looked pretty much abandoned." For the first time since she started talking, she looked at Tommy. There was something different in her eyes. That confidence was fading. "So we start to head into this little village, and all Hell breaks loose. I was in the second Humvee. The lead vehicle was hit by something, I still don't know what. It could have been an IED or an RPG. It doesn't matter.

Whatever hit them was powerful enough to blow the armored hummer off the road. Everybody in it was dead. The next thing I remember was being dragged through the desert." She stopped and looked down, away from the gun in pieces on the table.

"What happened next?" Tommy asked. He knew the look on her face. He'd seen it in himself, in so many others who had survived combat. She wasn't just remembering this, she was reliving it.

"They dragged me to a truck, I know that much, an old pickup. It was a red Toyota. The next thing I remember after that was waking up in a little mud brick building. I was tied to a chair. They had stripped me to my skivvies. Two men with AKs were standing by the door. They had keffiyehs over their faces. My head was bleeding, I could feel the warm blood running down my cheek. I didn't know if they had done it or if it had happened in the attack, but it was running pretty good, some of it had started to dry where it was dripping onto my leg." Her face changed again at the mention of blood. Something akin to a smile started to form on her lips before she became aware of it. Once she noticed, she quickly stifled the expression and continued. "I don't know how long I was there before he came in, but when that door opened, a rush of hot air came into the room with him. It was that hot, dry desert air, you know? The kind that lets you *know* that you're in a desert."

Tommy nodded.

"He walked right up to me and leaned down. His face was wrapped in a keffiyeh. His English was terrible, but I understood enough to know that he was interrogating me. I did what I was taught and gave him..."

"Name, rank, and serial number." Tommy interjected. It was the routine that American soldiers had learned as far back as any normal person could remember. Tommy knew that it was at least as old as the second World War, and probably older than that. It was also total bullshit.

"Exactly." Allison said, peering with one eye down the breach of the disassembled MP5. "What I got in return was the hardest punch I've ever taken, and an assurance that I'd *learn*. What happened over the next few months were beatings, every day. They made me sleep tied in the chair. If I had to piss or shit, I did it in the chair and sat in it. When my underwear got too dirty and smelly for them to stand, they stripped me naked and hosed me down with a power washer, then left me naked. The spray was so strong that the water broke my skin, embedded itself underneath, and took some of the hair off my body if they left it in one spot too long. Usually Muhammad, the man who was interrogating and beating me, would use a length of rubber hose on the soles of my feet, if I didn't cry out, he'd get something heavier, like a hot metal bar. If I didn't burst into tears when he scorch my feet with that, he'd use it to burn off my pubic hair. Of course," She slammed the breach back into the body of the gun with a force that startled Tommy. "burning off pussy hair is *not* an exact science. I still have the scars." She turned toward Tommy, that slight smile showing again before disappearing into a scowl. "Sometimes, I think just for fun, he'd hang me by my arms to the ceiling and whip my breasts and vagina with that rubber hose. Those times he'd invite all the men in the camp in to watch the American girl hanging there nude, crying, with blood droplets forming through the bruises on my tits while it dripped from where the hard rubber had split skin between my legs. They'd stand around and laugh and yell out suggestions to him while he beat me. Sometimes one of the other men would slide a long knife up between my legs and make me stand on my toes. If my legs gave out, I would've been impaled on it. I think their favorite part, though, was when I pissed myself."

She had reassembled the MP5 by now, and paused her story to hang it back on the wall. Glancing over her collection of weaponry, she chose an M16 and began disassembling it on the workbench.

Tommy shifted in his chair, even the thought was uncomfortable. He couldn't imagine retelling the memory, or for that matter, living it.

"After every beating or torture, this Muhammad would put me back in the chair and read from the Koran. This he could do in English pretty well, telling me all about a woman's place, and the importance of Jihad, and whatever else. I have a hard time keeping that part straight in my head." Allison picked up the clip she had taken out of the M16 and started pulling the bullets out one at a time and examining them. Tommy knew there was nothing to look at there, she was just doing anything she could to avoid eye contact. "I don't know how long this went on." She continued. "The days all blurred together. I figured eventually they'd get bored and kill me. I hoped they would, at least. One day, something changed, though."

"What was that?" Tommy asked.

"Muhammad came in for our usual daily beating and religious education, and he bought a box with him, it kinda looked like an old film projector."

"How so?"

"Well, it was made of wood, sitting on a tripod, and it had a lens on one end of it, like a projector. Muhammad called it the *Eye of Allah*. He said since I wouldn't listen to his teachings, I would have to learn this way. I was tied to my chair, as usual. He set the box on its stand across the room from me with the lens pointing at my face. He stepped to the side and turned a crank on the side of the box. I closed my eyes expecting some kind of bright light torture or something, but it didn't matter."

"Why not?" Tommy asked, leaning forward in his chair.

"Because there was no light. Just searing, mind blowing pain in every cell of my body. My eyes burned, my muscles contracted like I was being electrocuted. I don't know how else to explain it. It was like all the pain I'd suffered in my life had spread all at once to every fiber of my being. I could feel it in my brain. It was like nothing I'd ever felt before. I couldn't breathe. I was sweating profusely, and my sweat burned my skin. It was as though someone had set my blood on fire. Whatever fluids that were left in my body seemed to be boiling. I vomited, even though I hadn't had more than a cup of broth once a day for god knows how long. I vomited blood." She started pushing the bullets back into the magazine one at a time. A rhythmic click, click, click. "I don't know how long that thing was on, I think I blacked out, or blocked out part of it. All I know is that the sun was up when he started, and then it wasn't.

Allison finished putting the bullets back in the clip and moved over to a duffle bag that was sitting on the floor. She opened it up and started rummaging through its contents as she continued talking. "This went on every day in place of my beatings. I don't know how long, maybe months. One day I woke up in my chair, and the door was open. I was sitting there naked in an empty room. No guards, nothing. The Eye of Allah was gone, too. It took me a couple of minutes to realize that I wasn't tied to the chair anymore. I stood up on my own for the first time in months. I could barely bring myself to move, not knowing if someone was going to jump out and start the beatings all over again, punish me for moving. I noticed some clothing hanging near the open door. I had to force myself to move. I walked past the hook in the ceiling where they had hung me to whip and degrade me. It was the furthest I'd moved since I was taken. The clothes stank, they were dirty and used, but I had been naked for most of my captivity, and I didn't really care what the clothes smelled like, I just wanted to cover myself, to change myself from how they'd kept me." She was still kneeling down, but had given up any pretense of looking through the bag. Now she just stared into space.

"I felt the same way when I escaped from the Nazis." Tommy said. He thought about his experience in Austria, he had been on a mission, and it was all part of the plan, but that didn't keep him from having nightmares about that torture for months afterward.

"Yeah, your file said you were in the war, a spy or something." Allison said, still staring into space.

"What happened then?" Tommy asked.

"I walked outside. I walked into sunlight. It had been so long that I'd forgotten what it felt like. But I remembered very quickly." She finally turned and looked at Tommy. He was still sitting in the chair, but no longer leaning back. "When you've been kept out of the sun that long, and you walk directly into the desert light, you burn in minutes. I could feel it starting before I managed to find a scrap of cloth to throw over my head and face. My eyes burned from the intensity of the sun. I tried to shield them with my hands, but the light just reflected off the sand, so I just wrapped the scarf around my head and protected my eyes as best I could. I couldn't find any shoes, but my feet were so scarred from the beatings that I couldn't feel them being burned, anyway." She shifted to a cross-legged sitting position on the floor. "The whole place was abandoned. Well, when I say *whole place*, I mean the three huts out in the middle of nowhere in the desert. I headed west, I don't know why. It just seemed right. It was two days before I saw a road. I waited there for a full day. No one came. My throat was bone-dry. Hell, my body was bone-dry. I couldn't keep my mouth closed. My eyes were dry. I had trouble keeping me feet under me well enough to stand. But already I could feel something *different*."

"Different how?"

"Well, I could feel the dehydration. I could feel the pain in my stomach, my mind was wandering, I had a headache. All the signs of dehydration. But there was a drive. Like my mind was overruling my body. I could keep going through the pain, through the dehydration. I felt like I could keep going through anything. I don't know why, I felt *stronger*." She shifted her legs. Allison was sitting cross-legged on the concrete floor, her hands resting on her knees in an almost childlike position.

"How did you get out of the desert?" Tommy asked. He was fully drawn in by her story now, leaning forward in his chair with his elbows on his knees.

"Well," she continued, "after sitting at that road for a day, I kept heading west until I hit a highway." Allison uncrossed her legs and stood up, walking back toward the living area. "It had been three days since I left the terrorist camp, and I was starving. I could feel it. No matter what my mind was saying, I didn't know how long my body could go without food now, especially after the little bit of shit they had been feeding me."

Tommy heard water pouring into a pot. His view was partially blocked by the wire-grate walls, but it looked like she was cooking.

"Anyway, I got to the highway." She continued. "In reality, it wasn't much more than a two-lane road. I saw that it stretched out north and south as far as the eye could see, not a single building in either direction. I decided I was going to wait there for someone to pass. By now I was completely sunburned and wrapped from head to toe in fabric. No one would've mistaken me for an American soldier."

There was the sound of water boiling, then a metal spoon stirring a metal pot.

"I sat there for maybe four hours, give or take before I saw a truck. It was full of men with guns. I thought about hiding, thinking it could be the same men who had held me before, but I didn't have the energy and besides, out there, there's nowhere to hide."

Water poured into a sink. She was draining noodles, Tommy thought. Looking through the wall, he could see here standing over a sink, tossing them in a strainer.

"I stood up when the truck came by. The men were all in uniform, but not the Afghani uniforms. I knew what those looked like. They actually stopped when they saw me. A couple of them hopped out of the back of the truck while the rest kept their guns on me. They started questioning me, but not in Pashto, or Farsi or any of the other languages I'd heard in Afghanistan. Also," she paused, looking at Tommy through the grated wall, "ever been somewhere and just been able to tell, even though the people look the same, that they're *different?*"

Tommy nodded and gave a little grunt of agreement, not wanting to break her narrative.

"Well, that's how this was. They looked like the other soldiers I'd seen, but they carried themselves differently, almost more professional." She had transferred the noodles to a bowl and was mixing something with them, spices or something. "I answered them in English. I tried to tell them that I didn't know what they were asking me. They were standing a few feet away, their guns leveled at me. One of the men said something in broken English, I still don't know what, and then yelled over his shoulder to a man in the passenger seat of the truck. The man in the truck climbed out and walked over to me. This man looked different than the other soldiers. He had slightly lighter skin and his uniform was better fitted, obviously the leader. He asked me in pretty good English if I was American. I told him I was, that I was a soldier who had been captured and held about two-days' walk from here, to the east. There were all sorts of questions, what unit I was with, where I was stationed, why I wasn't in uniform, all sorts of things. I did my best to answer. The men who had taken me had taken my dog tags, so I had no proof of who I was. Finally after about twenty minutes of questions, he asked if it would be okay for him to search me for weapons. I realized then that I looked and came across every bit like a female suicide bomber. I told him he could, and he gave me a full pat down." She paused again and walked back around the wall. She had a mouthful of ramen noodles and a fork with another mouthful waiting.

"I eat and eat," she said, "but I never gain weight." She smiled. She swallowed her noodles and went on.

"When the leader was convinced that I was unarmed, they loaded me into the back of their truck with the soldiers. We drove for close to an hour before I saw a road sign. It said *Jacobabad 100 km*. The leader leaned out the window of the truck and yelled *Welcome to Pakistan* over the wind."

"You were in Pakistan? The whole time?" Tommy said, his eyes growing wide as he looked at the waifish woman sitting on the floor in front of him, eating cheap three minute ramen.

She swallowed another mouthful and continued. "Yeah. They figure I was being held at an old shepherd's station in the desert from the directions I gave them."

"So what happened then?"

"Once we got into the city, they drove me to their base. Apparently they had been out on maneuvers with units from western Pakistan all week and were just heading home when they found me. The commander, the one who spoke good English, said that that road isn't usually patrolled very much, and it was pure luck that they'd come across me." She finished her bowl of noodles and went back into the living area. Tommy could hear the sink running, and the bowl being set down. "Anyway, a female soldier kept guard over me while I showered at their barracks and then brought me some clean western-style clothes. They didn't fit very well. It was when I looked at her and then put on her clothes that I realized how thin I was. She was the same size I had been, but her clothes hung off me. When I finally got a medical exam a few days later, they told me that I was eighty-six pounds. When I shipped out, I was one hundred and thirty-five."

"Jesus."

"Yeah. So while I was getting cleaned up, the commander had called his bosses, who called their bosses, who called their bosses, who called the U.S. Embassy in Islamabad. They told them my name, and about three hours later an American helicopter landed outside the barracks. They brought a British Army doctor with them, since the embassy didn't have one available, and checked me out to make sure I could travel. After he gave the all clear, they flew me to the embassy."

"Then back to the U.S., I'm guessing."

"Well, yeah, after about a hundred hours of debriefing, a psych exam, a few more medical exams and a two week stop in Germany to regain my strength. Anyway, I had been gone about a year when I got back to the States. They took me straight to Walter Reed and admitted me to the psych ward to get me therapy so I could deal with my captivity and torture. Once I was there, I had time to think. I started having dark thoughts. I thought about killing my doctor, and it made me happy. I thought how easily I could murder the other patients. I started getting off on these thoughts, literally. I told the doctor about it, he said I could tell him anything. Instead of being understanding, he recommended that I be put in high security to keep me from hurting people. They sedated me, but no matter how high the dosage, it didn't work. My body just rejected the medicine and I stayed the same. Then I noticed it."

"Noticed what?"

"Well, I was eating one day, that shit food that they give you in the hospital. They wouldn't give me a fork or knife since I told the doctor about my thoughts, so I was eating with a spoon and drinking out of a plastic cup. I hit the cup with the back of my hand and as it started to fall, I caught it. Before it hit the table. I didn't mean to do it, but I caught it with the same hand. I moved so fast that it didn't spill. A few days later, I broke that same cup in my hand without thinking about it, I just squeezed."

"You were getting your strength back."

"I was getting stronger, getting faster. I never would have been able to catch that cup before. One of the nurses cut herself on something, and I saw her blood. They tried to keep me from seeing it, but I did. I couldn't sit still after that. I had to keep working out or my mind would wander, to places I didn't think I liked. I did pushups and situps, I ran in place. I could feel myself getting stronger, faster, sharper. There was nothing I could do to stop it. My mind was calculating things so fast, I felt like I could see through walls. I thought I was going crazy."

Tommy thought about his tears turning to blood in that church in Dublin so long ago, how it had made him stronger, how his mind had hardened around them. "Maybe you were a little bit. No one would fault you." He said.

Allison ignored him. "About a month later, they said I had a visitor. I thought it might be my family, maybe someone I served with. It wasn't. It was a man in a suit. He introduced himself as Agent Brinson of the NSA. He said he wanted to talk to me about what happened in Pakistan, about what they did to me."

"Agent Brinson?"

"The same one you met today." She said, staring at him.

Tommy realized that she had been staring at him for a few minutes now. He hadn't noticed if she'd blinked or not.

"He wanted to know about my torture, about the thing, he called it a *device*, that they had used on me. He wanted to know about any effects it might have had."

"Yeah, I bet he did."

"There was something strange going on. As soon as he walked into the meeting room, I wanted him. I wanted to seduce him, I wanted to fucking hurt him. I wanted to watch him bleed. I noticed that some of the male nurses and doctors were giving me similar feelings for a few months, but this was stronger. It was like a dimmer switch had been turned all the way up. I felt like he was a threat, and I knew how to deal with it. I felt confident. I felt sexy thinking about killing him."

Tommy just watched her. She sat on the floor watching him as she told her story. Now, as she spoke, her body shifted. Her back arched slightly. She was feeling that same feeling now.

"He asked me about it, and I did my best to answer. I tried to push those urges to the back of my mind. He had authority. I could sense it. Possibly even the authority to get me out of here, which was all I wanted. Then he said something that threw me."

"What was that?"

"He asked me what it had been like having a knife pressed against my vagina."

"That's a rough question."

"It was more than that. I hadn't told them about that, not even the doctor. I was embarrassed. I wasn't ready to share that yet. But he knew about it. I looked at him again, closer. I saw those eyes, light brown, cold eyes. I *knew* him, but not as Agent Brinson of the NSA. He was Muhammed."

"The same guy? How could you be sure?"

She looked at Tommy, her face a cold, blank stare. "You *never* forget." She said.

Tommy shifted under her glare. He knew she was dangerous, but until that look, after everything she'd told him, he finally realized how dangerous. He just hoped it wasn't directed at him.

"I went after him." She continued. "All those months of training had made me fast, but he knew it was coming. Before I could get across the table, two guards had grabbed me and injected me with something. It didn't knock me out, I doubt anything could now, but it weakened me enough. They dragged me back to my room and locked me in after giving me another shot. I couldn't do anything but lay there and think. Whatever they had given me had slowed down my body, but not my brain. I worked through it. Every detail. I went over everything again. It was him. It was our government. They tortured me. They scarred me. They turned that device on me. When I thought about the device, it all made sense. The strength, the reflexes, the sick thoughts. That thing had changed me. It had turned me into this." She gestured to herself. "They made me into this. I decided right then that I had to get out. I had to find out why, and I had to make them pay. That's when the orderly came into my room."

"The one you killed?"

"He was the first. I'm guessing Brinson told you the story?"

"You suffocated him with his own dick."

Allison smiled and shifted her hips again. "Yeah, I did. He deserved it. That's what you get for trying to take advantage of a sedated patient. That's when I figured out that I could physically overpower anything in my system."

"Good skill to have."

"Usually. Makes getting drunk kinda boring, though." She said. "Anyway, I escaped that night. I had to kill one of the inmate trustees to get out, and I almost lost it on that one. I was almost too turned on. But I got out, and started looking."

"And that led you here?"

Allison stood up and walked to the computer. She started to move the mouse and click folders, moving things around. Tommy saw her from the side now, she was only five feet away. Standing there in a tank top and skin tight black jeans, she didn't look like a killer. "Eventually. It took a lot for me to get it under control. To get myself under control. But I did, more or less." She smiled at Tommy. It was that same dark smile she'd flashed at him before. "I had to rob, steal, and kill to get what I needed, but I finally found out that he was in Pittsburgh, that his offices were here.

I found out they were using criminals to test the devices, to find their limits. I managed to get ahold of the documents I've shown you. That's how I learned what they were trying to do to me. I don't understand all of it, but I understand enough about myself. I know that they tried to turn me into a killer, but they didn't expect the side effects."

"Which are?"

"I get off on destruction, on death, on pain." She gripped the table with her hands, her back arching again. "I used to save lives, diffuse bombs, protect people. Now, there's nothing sexier to me than making people suffer and die." Allison looked off into the distance, over the computer desk. She stared into the blackness for a moment, then pulled herself back to the laptop monitor. "Here." She said, pulling a flash drive out of the laptop. "This is what I have so far. Like I said, I can only make sense of some of it. You've been dealing with this stuff longer than I have, you might be able to figure it out." She handed Tommy the flash drive and paused for a second still holding it. She stared at him with that smile. "And maybe," she added, "you can find your Maxwell Ash in there somewhere. Some people are only referred to by code names."

Tommy pulled his hand away, taking the flash drive and breaking contact. Allison turned and walked back to the living area, slipping on her body armor and a clean turtleneck. She grabbed the truck keys off the workbench and turned to him again.

"I'd better leave you back where I found you. If we do it right, they won't pick you up on the cameras until you walk out of the alley, and it'll give Brinson something to wonder about." She started walking toward the truck, and Tommy followed.

CHAPTER 5

She dropped him back off in the alley after more extremely defensive driving. The wind was blowing colder off the rivers now, and he turned up the collar of his overcoat as he stepped into the sidewalk. Tommy's car was maybe ten blocks from here, and the night was alive with people.

He walked through the crowds of chattering, oblivious shapes with his head down. His run-in with Agent Brinson had made him even more aware that he was being watched, but now it was worse than he thought. *Everyone* was being watched. He wondered if these people he was passing ever considered what all those cameras they passed every day were for. Probably not. Most people, even people with secrets, didn't really think that they'd be found out. Criminals thought all cops were stupid, and if they just kept their heads down, no one would notice what they were planning. They didn't know that there were others out there, people with technology and The Patriot Act on their side, who were looking for the ones with their heads down, looking for the quiet indicators, looking for people who were keeping their noses clean.

Tommy felt light headed. As he walked, his vision blurred. He wondered for a moment if the shot to the head he took when that car hit him had done more damage than he realized. He lifted his face into the cold wind. Winding through the dark mass of people on the sidewalk, he found the wall. He could smell soot and ash as he leaned up against it. He ran his hands over his coat, feeling the cold comfort of the revolver handles through the material as his heart thumped in his chest. Something was wrong. He was being followed. He knew it like never before.

Tommy looked down the street. Carriages rolled along the cobblestone as well dressed men and women walked along the sidewalk. He saw a man across the street. He was in a tweed coat and trousers. He had a thick mustache and a bowler hat. He leered at Tommy. A Pinkerton. How had they found him so quickly? He'd only been in town for a day.

Tommy turned his head and saw another. Standing there under the gaslight in the cold. Watching him, though he tried to conceal himself behind the crowd, Tommy could see him. Everywhere he looked, there were more of them. The mill bosses must have a spy in the union. That's the only way they could know about Tommy so quickly. He pushed himself up the wall and headed down the street to where he'd left his hire cab. He only had a few blocks to go now, but they were following him. If they started trouble now, he was outnumbered. He'd been practicing with the Colt, but he wasn't good enough to take on more than two men if it came down to pulling iron.

Men shouted as he pushed his way through the crowd. He tried to apologize, but he had to get away from these men before they knew he was onto them. Tommy turned a corner, making sure to stay on the busier streets, hoping he'd lose them in the crowd. He stopped and looked in a shop window, all decorated for Christmas with the newest dresses for ladies and toys for the little ones. One of those big department stores he still hadn't gotten used to in his three years in America. He saw a dress and a train. It made him think of his wife and little boy.

A reflection in the glass caught his eye. Another man, standing at a hack stand. He was pretending to read a paper, but he kept looking over the top of it at Tommy. Another Pinkerton.

They were still on him. The front page of the paper read: *Homestead Strike Stretches Into Second Month.*

That was why he was here. Not his baby, not his wife. He was here to kill a man. A Pinkerton. Maxwell Ash. He'd gone after the families of the strike leaders. Threatened women and children. Burned down houses. Was one of these men following him Ash? He didn't know. He did know that he wasn't ready for a fight. Ash was a killer, and Tommy was at a disadvantage right now.

Tommy hadn't even met with the strike leaders yet. He was supposed to meet them tomorrow. But he already had heat on him. He wondered if he should call the whole thing off. Just leave. They hadn't paid him yet, they didn't know what he looked like, just his reputation. He could disappear again, like he did when he left Australia. He could leave in the morning, and no one would ever know he'd shown up at all.

It was a keen thought. But obviously, the Pinkertons already knew. Would they stop hunting him if he left? Not based on their reputation. They'd keep after him until they knew he wasn't a threat. Tommy was still a wanted man in England. He had no doubt the Pinkies knew that. All they had to do was catch him and they'd get the reward, and he'd get the gallows for sure this time.

Tommy turned and kept walking up the slippery cobblestone sidewalk. A hack passed by, splashing dark grey water and ice on his trousers. He pretended to scratch his back, feeling the handle of the Colt stuck in his belt. It was no comfort.

All at once he could see it. The hack he'd asked to wait while he went and got cleaned up. It was sitting there right where he'd left it. The driver saw him and hopped back up, taking the reigns in his hand and picking the whip up from his seat. Two blocks. Just two blocks. Tommy stopped and pretended to check the watch he had stolen from the British officer. He turned and looked back up the street as though he was looking for a public clock to set by. He saw three of the Pinkerton men making their way up the street, trying to look as inconspicuous as possible. They were less than a block away. Tommy pushed the button on the side of his watch.

Everything stopped around him. The snow hung in the air like in a photograph. He watched the Pinkerton men stop mid-stride. One of them was caught staring right at Tommy. He had two minutes if he didn't push the button again. That's how it worked. He didn't know why, it just did.

There was a dull grey snowflake hanging in the air in front of him. Tommy flicked it with his finger. It bounced to the side a few inches and then wobbled back to where it started. That was how it worked. He could move, but he couldn't move anything around him. It would always go back where it was when he stopped time.

Tommy looked at the second hand on the watch. He had fifty eight seconds left. Tommy jogged up the street and hit the button again, restarting time. He told the driver to take him to the boarding house he'd checked into this morning. The driver called to the horses and they set off north.

Tommy watched as the Pinkerton men ran down the street toward his cab, breaking their cover. He slid down in the seat of the enclosed carriage for the rest of the ride.

When he got to the boarding house, he hopped out and noticed a man standing in a doorway across the street smoking a pipe. He was thin, wearing black leather gloves and smoking a pipe. The glow of the pipe in the darkness gave him away. Tommy turned and walked into the building, pretending not to notice.

Getting to his room, Tommy slammed and locked the door. He slid off his overcoat and felt light headed again. He reached for the gun in the belt of his pants, then remembered that he had them in shoulder holsters now. He had to sit down.

He stumbled to the cot on shaking legs and flopped down. He reached for the bottle of whisky on the floor and saw that his hands were shaking violently.

Too much past. Too many pasts. Tommy took a deep swig of the bottle and set it on the floor. He covered his face with his shaking hands. His wife and child. Katrina Liu. Scotty. So many others. He couldn't remember all their names, or he never bothered to learn them. So many ghosts, and every one a demon. Tommy picked the bottle back up and took another deep swig.

The next morning, Tommy was up early. The one advantage to his strange situation was that he never got a hangover. His body rejected the alcohol's effects on his cells. After a couple of hours, it simply went away.

He was flipping through the files Allison had given him on a little netbook he'd bought this morning. The guy wanted to sell him the floor model, but Tommy insisted on having one that hadn't been touched. He struggled not to use the phrase *forensically clean* with the idiot behind the counter, but Tommy managed to get his point across without causing too much of a scene in the store.

The thumb drive contained thousands of pages. Photographs and scanned copies of faded documents dating back to the late eighteen seventies. Tommy was still a little kid in Ireland when some of this information was collected. There were no names, very little even written in the first person except a couple of short personal letters from Adalai Merrick. One was a letter to his daughter and son in law congratulating them on the birth of their daughter, another a short note to someone unnamed, stating that Merrick was leaving England, and that his property was to be sold, and his personal property burned, excluding his Victoria Cross, which was to be returned to the government as though he'd died. Tommy knew that Merrick had been a national hero in England after the Crimean War, but he had no idea the guy had received a VC for it.

The next entry was a short note about Merrick's disappearance. It stated that Merrick was nowhere to be found, and Eliza was running his watch shop. The government had been watching them since they entered the country. Why didn't they intervene when the Khlysti came after Eliza? There was surveillance on her the whole time. They had detailed files on her movements in the time between Adalai's disappearance and the night on the edge of the canal when Tommy and Eliza had their run-in with Rasputin and his men.

But there was something new here. Tommy thought he knew everything about that night. He had gone over it in painful detail. Over and over again his mind ran through it, whether Tommy wanted to or not. He had a perfect memory of it. Every moment, every step he took trying to lead Eliza to safety. In the years since, he'd gone over all of it, trying to see if there was anything he could have done differently. He'd gone back to the site after he healed. Back then, before his body had adjusted to its new situation, it took him longer to heal. It was probably four months before he was mobile enough to go back there. There was no evidence, in his mind or at the scene, of anyone other than Tommy, Eliza, Rasputin, and his two men having been there.

But now, he was reading a report from a Secret Service agent who arrived just after the attack. He claimed that there had been a witness. The witness was a tall man with a thick mustache who had a severely wounded right hand and identified himself as a Pinkerton agent from Pittsburgh. Then he saw the name. *Maxwell Ash*.

Ash was there. He followed Tommy from Pittsburgh to Buffalo. He was hunting. Tommy was in Buffalo for four months before that night on the canal. This document said that Ash had been in Buffalo for two months following Tommy.

Tommy thought he'd left Ash behind in Pittsburgh. He thought that wounding Ash and killing his partner had been enough to get ahead of him. Ash knew where he was the whole time, and didn't take him down. Why not? If Ash just wanted him dead, why would he wait so long? Tommy had let his guard down in Buffalo after a couple months. Ash could've gotten the drop on Tommy any time he wanted. But he didn't. What was Ash planning back then?

He kept going through the documents. They were organized by year and subject. The file on Tommy started on that night. There was no file on Ash at all. He just disappeared after that one connection. How could they have so many details of everyone who was ever connected to the devices, going back over a century, but nothing on him? Ash was there, Ash was immortal, just like Tommy and Rasputin. Tommy had seen him in person just a year ago. The bastard had left a photograph of Tommy from Pittsburgh in Tommy's hotel room in Baton Rouge. Maxwell Ash was hunting him again. Just like before. But why had he waited so long? He'd had a hundred years to find him. Tommy had laid low, but not nearly *that* low. If Ash had wanted to find him, he could've.

Thousands of pages. Tommy kept reading. He started on the Eliza Merrick file. They had details that Tommy didn't have. Hell, they had details that Adalai Merrick himself probably didn't have. There were notes in there about where she lived, who she associated with, what she ate, her political leanings. There were inventories of the contents of her homes and apartments, her offices when she ran businesses, everything. They were looking for something. There was mention of a codex. They never found it, but they kept looking. For almost fifty years, they searched her luggage when she travelled, they replaced her moving men and rummaged through her boxes when she moved.

But the trail on her went cold in nineteen forty six. She got on a train in Texas, and never got off. There were four government agents on the train, and more at every stop. Eliza Merrick had more security around her than the President. She just disappeared from history.

What seemed to bother whoever wrote this report more than that, though, was that they never found the codex. A book. They weren't looking for her, they thought she had this book. What was so important about the book?

Tommy flipped through page after page of files until he found it. The Merrick Codex. The entry said that they weren't even sure if it existed, but Rasputin had told them that Adalai Merrick, in the time he was a prisoner of war and under Rasputin's control in the Crimea, had started collecting details on all of the devices they had. He knew their makers. He got ahold of the men's personal papers, journals and research. Merrick had everything. According to the files, when

Merrick escaped the Russians, he took all of the papers with him.

Burn all of his personal papers. That was what Merrick had told his friend. He didn't want the documents getting into the wrong hands. Merrick had been collecting information on watchmakers and their creations since before Tommy was born. Before so much information was destroyed in World War Two. He'd had access to documents about these things that Tommy could have only dreamed of.

The file went on to state that Merrick had allegedly collected the greatest store of information on devices in the world. Possibly ever. No wonder the government wanted the book. If it was real, and they got ahold of it, they could recreate the devices.

But if the book had existed, no one had ever seen it, and the only person who might know its whereabouts disappeared sixty seven years ago.

Tommy kept looking for details on Ash, but there was nothing. No details at all. They had everything on Tommy, including his last meeting with Father Daniel the day he left Buffalo, but nothing on Ash being there. Tommy knew he was there. He'd seen him. He didn't recognize him at the time, but looking back on it, Ash watched him leave the church, watched him pull away in his Jag.

Ash was there, but the government men didn't see him.

Tommy had to find Ash. He was involved. He was the reason Tommy was in Pittsburgh. Somehow, he was involved with the crimes that used devices. He closed the netbook and pulled out the flash drive. Looking around the room, he saw all the red strings. They chased each other around the room, back to the map. They had been there for months, growing into an ever-larger web. There had to be some connection. Start at the base. That's how this works. You follow the web and that will lead you to the spider. Ash *was* a spider. He always had been. So what was the connection? Tommy let his eyes pass over the walls. He'd gone through these men's lives hundreds of times. He knew all of their friends, their family, their known associates, everyone. He knew who they bunked with when they were locked up, he knew where they worked when they were on parole. He'd stolen every possible bit of official information he could get ahold of.

His eyes followed the details of their lives. He followed from one to the next. A father and son, brothers, details stacked on details in his mind. Was there anything, anything at all that connected these men to each other? Some, yes, but not enough of them to explain the spread of devices. Tommy flipped through the pages in his mind. Nothing in their personal lives, nothing in the prison system, none of them worked at the same places on parole, nothing.

Tommy sat upright in his chair. *Parole.* Every single one of them was on parole. He jumped out of his chair and rummaged through the files on the small table near the desk. He found a name. The file fell to the floor and he picked up the next one on the pile. Same name. He looked at one of the mugshots on the wall. Crossing the small room, he pulled the corresponding file out of a stack, sending the rest of the stack onto the floor in a disorganized pile. Same name, again.

He started frantically digging through the folders. How could he have missed it. Every one of them, every single one! The same name every time. Tommy slumped back in his chair fifteen minutes later. The room was littered with loose pages from the files he'd so meticulously collected. The same name. And he'd missed it. All these months and the answer had been right under his nose.

The parole officer. The goddamn parole officer. Gary Collette. Same one. All these dead ex cons had the same parole officer. He couldn't believe he'd missed it. All these months looking over the files, reading, collating, cross-referencing, re-reading. And he missed the fact that was right in front of his face.

A quick phone call to the parole offices told Tommy that the guy had retired. He pulled out his laptop and did a quick search for the name. The parole officer's phone number didn't come up, he was probably unlisted. It did, however, bring up his current employer. Gary Collette was listed as a security specialist with a private firm downtown. Tommy scratched down the address on a sheet of paper, and grabbed his coat and guns. As he slammed the door, he wondered what he'd do when he got to the building. A private security company was bound to have some pretty decent guards, and he wasn't looking for a fight. He wanted information. Could he bluff his way in?

He was over thinking it. It was afternoon already, by the time he got into the city, the office might be closed, anyway. He hoped it wasn't. In an office building full of people, you can blend in with a crowd, get on and off elevators without being noticed, even get through secured doors. In an empty building, it's just you and the security guards.

As Tommy drove into the city, his phone rang. He didn't recognize the number, but now it could be anyone. Brinson most likely knew his number, Allison wouldn't have any trouble figuring it out, for sure.

Tommy picked up the phone and pressed talk.

"Hello?"

"Mr. McKinney. It's been a while."

Tommy thought the voice sounded familiar, but between a bad connection and the roar of a straight six with no catalytic converter, he couldn't quite tell.

"Who is this?" Tommy said.

"This is Brother Marcus, Tommy."

Motherfucker. How did that bastard get his phone number if not from Father Daniel? He was right. Daniel was trying to bring him in, trying to protect the Church's secret.

"Before you assume anything, I didn't get this number from your friend Daniel. I asked, even politely, but he told me he didn't have it."

Was he telling the truth, or trying to protect his mole?

"What do you want, Marcus?"

"It's not what I want, Mr. McKinney. It's what my order, what the Church wants." Tommy could hear the venom in his voice even through the bad connection.

"Well, you know me, Marcus. Anything for the Church." Tommy made no attempt to hide his sarcasm. If Marcus represented the whole church now, Tommy didn't want any part of it.

"I've gotten some information that you're still looking into what we discussed in Baton Rouge. I'm calling to tell you to stop now."

"Trying to warn me off, Marcus? What, am I getting too close to your little secret?"

"You're meddling in things, and with people that are beyond your scope, McKinney. Don't you realize that? How do you think I got your number? We are the Catholic Church. Our power is great and far-reaching."

"I figured you just looked me up. I'm not real worried about you right now, Marcus. You send your little priests to try and persuade me, do whatever you like. You might think I'm stupid, but even I know that Inquisitors aren't allowed to draw blood."

"Oh, yes. You're little hunting trip in Pittsburgh. How's that going for you? Did you find your ghost? And you're absolutely right, I can't draw your blood. But that doesn't mean I can't make your life Hell. You keep looking into things that are none of your business, and I'll make sure you end up alone in this world, with *nothing*."

The line went dead. What did Marcus mean, "nothing?" Tommy had nothing now. No name, no family, and if he was right and Father Daniel had betrayed him: no friends.

CHAPTER 6

Tommy pulled the car into a parking space on the side of the road. He'd managed to park just outside PPG Place. The office was on the fortieth floor of the building right in front of him, The great black-mirrored Gothic style tower known as PPG One. It was one of a pair, matching monuments to one of the industries that built the modern city, in fact, most modern American cities, Pittsburgh Paint and Glass.

There was a man standing a few blocks away. He looked young, though Tommy couldn't really make out his face. He stood there in the partial shadows like an omen. He didn't have the cut of a government agent. His hands were in his pockets, swaying gently back and forth on his heels.

Tommy thought he looked familiar, but couldn't place him. One thing seemed sure, though. He was watching Tommy.

Tommy pushed the thought to the back of his mind. There was nothing he could do about it right now. He had to get inside and see what he could find out about the parole officer. He needed to know what connection he had to Ash. He needed answers.

Walking into the glass and marble lobby, Tommy looked for the directory. These building were so big, they had to have one. Once he found it, the security company was easy to locate. They didn't have their name on the wall, but the entire fortieth floor was absent from the list. Tommy figured that if they were a decent security firm, they'd want to keep their presence as quite as possible. Finding them in the phone book was one thing, most people would just call. But if they were on the wall in the building's directory, then anyone who happened into the lobby would know right where to find them. People looking for other things would probably never notice that the fortieth floor was missing from the list, they would be too concerned with finding what they were looking for.

He walked over to the bank of elevators. The lobby guard barely gave him a second look. It wasn't uncommon for people to come and go from offices in the evening, and dressed in a suit,

Tommy looked like any normal businessman coming in to finish up paperwork after hours.

Luckily, the elevator wasn't key code protected. Tommy pushed the button for the fortieth floor and the car started to rise. He had time to think now, time to consider what to do next. He didn't really have a plan. He hadn't had one in several months. He was playing things by ear these days. Granted, so far it hadn't worked out too well. He needed to stop and think, but his mind wouldn't. He just kept driving on, further and further into whatever this situation really was. At this point, he didn't know if any of it was real or if he was imagining everything about Ash. He knew the picture was real, he knew from the government documents that Ash had been there that night, the night everything had changed. But now? No one involved seemed to know anything about him. It was like he was a mirage.

From what Tommy remembered, he was just that. The man was smart, possibly smart enough to make himself disappear. Hell, Tommy did, why couldn't Ash? The elevator started to slow around the thirty-seventh floor. Tommy didn't know what would be on the other side of the door. His hands slid down his jacket, feeling the butts of his twin Colts. He took a deep breath.

The doors opened. Nothing. No guards, no cameras. A wall to the right, a hallway to the left. Tommy followed the hallway to the corner of the building. It made two right turns. Following it around, he finally came to a large, heavy looking door with a guard desk in front of it. There was a long bank of windows on his left. The guard looked up from his computer screen as Tommy approached.

"Can I help you?" He asked warily.

"I'm John Smith, I have an appointment." Tommy said.

"No, you don't. These offices close at six p.m. No appointments after five thirty." The guard said. He turned his body so that his legs were free of the desk. "Now, if you'll kindly get back on the elevator." The guard motioned down the hallway behind Tommy.

"But, I just need to see them for a second. I'm trying to get a job here." Tommy said, leaning in slightly.

"No positions available." The guard said, standing up. He cleared six feet by at least five inches, and he looked like he knew what to do with it. "Now go back down the hall, and leave the building." He again pointed behind Tommy.

Tommy tried to push by. "But I just want to talk to them for a second!"

The guard pushed Tommy back. "Sir, leave the building now, or I'll use force."

This guard had more self control than most. Tommy probably wasn't the first person to wander up here, and the guy knew how to handle it, better than most.

He had to get through that door. It had a keypad entry system, and the guard knew the pass code, Tommy was sure of it. He only had a split second to decide. If he left, he might never find out what was going on. If he tried to push through, he could end up arrested or out a window.

Tommy swung with everything he had. The guard tried to duck out of the way. The punch landed on the man's temple instead of his chin. A right followed the left. Tommy again connected. This time he hit his target. The guard's head snapped around on his neck. He was dazed, but only for a second. Tommy saw him reach into the back of his pants. He expected the guard to produce a baton or taser. Instead he pulled out a six inch tactical knife. The kind special forces carry.

He came at Tommy with the knife. The first swing was wild, a dazed, angry slash. Tommy easily dodged it. The second was more collected, a sharp jab toward Tommy's stomach. Tommy hopped backward to keep out of reach of the blade.

As the guard reared his arm back for another swing, Tommy saw an opportunity.

Ducking his head, Tommy charged the guard, his shoulder making contact just under the bigger man's ribs. He felt the air go out of the man as the knife blade clinked on the polished floor. The force of the impact carried both of them into the secured door. The man crumpled toward the floor gasping for breath as Tommy stood up.

"Are you gonna let me in?" Tommy said.

The guard shook his head, fighting to get his breath back. Tommy pulled the man from the floor and pushed him up against the bank of windows.

"Are you gonna let me in?" Tommy said again, his voice taking on a dry, menacing tone.

"Not on your life." The guard managed to cough out.

Tommy pulled the man off the glass and slammed him back into it. Spiderwebs shot through the entire width of the sheet of safety glass. Blood began to drip from the window behind the big man's head. The broken edges of the safety glass had cut him, deep.

"Are you gonna let me in?" Tommy said again.

The guard shook his head. Blood sprayed the cracked window and floor.

Tommy slammed him into the glass again. This time, the entire window gave way, falling in one bent piece to the sidewalk below. The upper half of the guard's body hung out of the hole. Now there was nothing between the guard and eternity but Tommy's grip on his collar.

"Are you going to let me in?" Tommy said, his voice controlled, almost cold.

The guard just smiled. He knew Tommy couldn't get in without him. If he threw him out of the window, Tommy would lose. If he walked away now, he'd lose. The guard thought he had checkmate.

Tommy pulled the man back in and threw him against the wall. The guard managed to keep his feet, but there was no fight left in him. Picking up the knife from where it had landed, Tommy walked over to him and pressed the tip of the blade into the man's stomach.

"Let me through that door." Tommy said.

"No." The guard coughed. As he shook his head, he left smears of blood along the wall behind him.

Tommy jabbed the blade up under the man's ribs. The guard's eyes opened wide as the razor sharp edge found its mark. Over and over Tommy jabbed, pushing the blade up under the ribs into the vital organs. Tommy stopped when the man started to slide down the wall and the blood on his hands made the handle of the knife too slick to keep a grip.

Tommy caught the guard as he fell. Taking the weight of the dead man on his shoulder, he maneuvered the body back into the chair, sitting up. It took a little work, but the man just looked like he was sleeping at the desk. He couldn't do anything about the blood on the wall or the missing window, but at least he might be able to buy a few minutes.

He cleaned the knife off with his handkerchief and slid it back into its sheath on the guard's belt then wiped his own hands. He'd gotten some blood on his shoes and shirt cuffs, but nothing a casual observer would notice. As long as he kept his coat on, he should be able to get back to his room without causing suspicion.

As he rode the elevator back to the lobby, he thought on the next step. What could he do now? Once they found that guard, the whole building would be full of cops. Worse, the security company would be on high alert, and judging from the door guard, they weren't your average home security system company. They were a professional outfit, either bodyguards or mercenaries, or both. Either way, there was no way he was getting back into that office.

The doors opened in the lobby. Tommy walked past the guard and nodded, trying to look as nonchalant as possible. He made it through the doors and noticed a black SUV parked behind his Jag. Leaning up against it was a small figure in black.

"They wouldn't let you in?" Allison said, smiling.

"No, and now I've got no leads on Ash at all. How did you know I'd be here?" Tommy said, walking to his car.

"Oh, I didn't until I saw the Jag. I have my own business here." She looked over the silver classic. "Kind of a conspicuous car, don't you think?"

"It's the one thing I allow myself. A blacked out SUV doesn't draw any attention?" Tommy said, motioning to her truck.

"Well, yeah, but people see a truck like this and figure it's government. The last thing they want to do is get involved." She said.

"Good point." Tommy said, opening the door to his car.

"Where are you going?" Allison asked.

"To try and find another link to lead me to Ash. I'm not getting into that office." Tommy said.

"Secure door? Numeric keypad?" Allison asked.

"Yeah, why?"

"All you had to do was ask." She said.

Allison pulled something from behind her back. It looked like the handle from a rifle with a red trigger attached. She pulled the trigger.

The forty-first floor of the office building exploded. Fire raged for a split second from the windows. Shards of glass rained down. Tommy turned his back to the chaos to protect himself from flying debris. Car alarms sounded everywhere. Allison calmly clicked hers off.

"Ampho." She said, smiling. "Slow speed explosive. Not the most delicate thing in the world, but it makes a hell of a boom. And that was a particularly good one." Allison started running toward the building. Tommy followed.

"What the fuck is wrong with you?" He screamed.

"When there's a fire, all automatic doors reset to unlock. It's a security precaution built in to the buildings to allow firemen access." She said.

As they reached the lobby, all hell was breaking loose. The guard was on the phone, most likely with the police or fire department. There were sprinklers going off, and people, the few who were left in the building, were coming down the stairs. Allison ran to the elevator.

"The elevator?" Tommy said. "How do you know it's still working?"

"I set the explosives at the windows." Allison said as they got on. "They made a big boom and set off the alarms, but didn't do much damage." She pushed the button and the doors closed.

"You could've started a small fire." Tommy said after several seconds of silence.

"Where's the fun in that?" Allison said, her eyes gleaming.

The doors opened at the fortieth floor. As they stepped into the hallway, Tommy could hear sirens in the distance.

"We've got a few minutes until they get up here." Allison said. "They're going to go floor to floor checking everything. They're going to treat this as a terrorist attack."

"Why would they do that?" Tommy asked.

She stared at him. "Seriously? I just set off eighty pounds of high explosive in the tallest building in the city. What would you call it?"

"Psychopathic, but then I know you." Tommy said.

"Aww, you do, don't you?" Allison said, her mouth pressing into a pout. "Come on, we don't have all day." She ran down the hall toward the guard desk.

Tommy followed.

Allison stopped at the end of the hall, staring at the guard slumped over in his chair. "That blast was on the next floor up. What happened to him?" She said.

"I did." Tommy responded, walking past her toward the security door.

Allison examined the guard's body. Her eyes lingered over the multiple stab wounds in the guard's chest. "And you call *me* psychopathic?" She said.

Tommy just glanced over his shoulder as he open the now unlocked security door and walked into the office. He had no response. Killing the guard was unnecessary. It was messy and brutal. There was no excuse for leaving a calling card like that.

Walking into the office, all he could hear was the wail of the fire alarm. His clothes were soaked through now by the sprinkler system. Allison hurried to the back of the office where a long bank of filing cabinets stood against the wall. Tommy followed her, hoping that they were looking for the same thing.

"You said you had business here." He said, watching her flip through a deep row of files.

"Yeah," She said, "This security company is a front for the NSA, for Brinson. I'm trying to find files on their current operations. If you're going to find any information on Ash, this is probably the place."

Tommy took the hint and started digging through the files. He scanned them quickly, looking for names, descriptions, anything.

Meanwhile, Allison had apparently found what she was looking for. She took a sheet of paper over to a computer and started typing.

Tommy kept going through the files. There was nothing, no mention of either Ash or Rasputin. It was like they'd never existed. Tommy knew they had, he'd seen files on Rasputin in the data Allison had given him earlier.

Allison pulled a small flash drive out of her pocket. Pushing it into a slot on the computer, she typed a bit more and started looking around. The computer screen changed, a long blue bar in a gray box indicated that files were being transferred.

Tommy went back to scanning through the files. There was nothing on Ash. Nothing at all, not even the mention of another immortal like him. From what he could scan quickly, they didn't even have any files on Rasputin, and Allison had confirmed they were working with him. He saw one labeled *The Merrick Codex*. He grabbed this and folded the manila folder up into his jacket pocket.

Allison yelled from across the room. "We've got maybe five more minutes before the firemen get to this floor. They'll lock this building down faster than you can say boo."

Tommy nodded. This meant get out now. Tommy scanned a few more files in the drawer he had open and then slid it shut, wiping down the handle to remove his fingerprints. No reason to let Brinson know he had been there.

When he turned, Allison was standing next to him. She motioned with her head toward the door and Tommy followed her out. As they got to the elevator in the hall, they could hear the firemen in the stairwell. The elevator doors closed just as the firemen burst through the fire door and started sweeping the floor.

When they arrived in the lobby, they stepped into chaos. There were police in riot gear everywhere. Firemen and people in suits shouting commands, EMTs ready to deal with any injuries.

Allison slumped over and started limping. Tommy took her lead and wrapped his arm over her shoulder, as though helping her walk. A fireman ran up to them.

"How bad is she hurt?" He said.

"It's not bad, I twisted my ankle trying to get down the stairs." She patted Tommy on the chest. "He got me in the elevator to get me down."

"Okay." The fireman said. "If you want medical attention, there are ambulances outside." He looked at Tommy. "Can you get her out there yourself?"

"Yeah." Tommy said. "She's light."

The fireman stepped out of the way and motioned Tommy with a hand toward the door. At

~ 123 ~

the same time he made a hand motion to the policemen near the door. They opened up the glass doors and ushered Tommy and Allison through onto the street.

After convincing a couple of EMTs that Allison didn't need medical care, they crossed the street to their cars. Allison suggested that they drive a few blocks and reconvene, to get out of the cordoned-off area.

Tommy followed her to a parking lot about five blocks away. He could still hear the sirens as more and more law enforcement and rescue teams showed up at what looked for all the world like a terrorist attack.

When Tommy got out of the car, Allison was standing next to her truck, waiting.

"That was a nice move in the lobby." He said, walking toward her truck.

"Ahh, the damsel in distress. No fireman can resist it." Allison said, smiling. "That move can get you into more government buildings than all the pass codes in the world." She looked him in the eye. "Did you find what you were looking for?"

Tommy looked down. "No. There was nothing on Ash in there at all. It's like he never existed, like he hasn't been on their radar since the eighteen nineties."

"Well, maybe he did die. Maybe he died a long time ago. People *do* die, you know."

"Not people like Maxwell Ash. Even if he wasn't immortal, that evil sonofabitch would live forever. I'll have to find the link to him somewhere else."

"Well, good luck with that." Allison said, opening the door to her SUV. "In the meantime, I'll be lying low for a bit. It won't take Agent Brinson long to realize that I did this." She swung herself up into the truck and started the engine. "See you around, Tommy." She said, pulling the door closed and slamming the big truck into gear. The tires squealed as she raced out of the parking lot and around the corner, completely ignoring the red light at the intersection.

Tommy walked back to his Jag as several fire trucks and police cars flew past at top speed. They were all headed toward PPG Place. None of them were even remotely concerned with the businessman getting into his car in a darkened parking lot.

Tommy had learned, over years and years of practice, that people only see what they want to see. The human brain could only handle so much information at one time. It looks for motion, for immediate threats, for loud noises and danger.

Don't make loud noises, don't be threatening, don't move, and you won't get noticed. Simple as that. If you can make a threat appear somewhere else, you're even better off. Everyone looks toward the burning building, the gunshots, the sound of a car crash. No one watches the quiet man behind them with the gun under his coat.

That's how he'd made it this far. Letting people look at the threats in other places. Never appearing to be a threat himself. He wondered if Ash was doing the same thing: Hiding himself deep under the clear and obvious threat of the NSA. Was he working in the shadows even now, watching everything that happened and waiting to make his move?

The NSA. Tommy had almost forgotten for a second about Brinson and his cameras. He looked around at the buildings on all sides of him as he slid behind the wheel of the Jag and started the engine.

CHAPTER 7

After parking the car behind the building, Tommy made his way up to his little room and locked the door behind him. He lowered the blinds after checking the quiet wintery street. It seemed so long since Buffalo. In reality it had been just over a year, but to him it felt like an eternity. He'd had a life there, such as it was. He'd had Scotty, and paying work. It was a simple life. He'd worked toward finding a cure for his condition in his free time. He'd managed more or less to keep the devices out of the hands of people who shouldn't have them. Occasionally, he'd even helped people.

Now, he was a refugee on a mission of destruction. He couldn't even count how many people he'd killed at this point, but he knew his tally with God was deep in the red. He also knew he should care, but he didn't. He missed the old building on Perry Street. It had been his home for close to a hundred years. Now it was a burned out hulk, like most of the rest of the old First Ward. He'd done it himself. Burned down his own home so no one could find evidence of who he really was.

He'd left everything behind. For what? For this? He looked around his rented room. He'd been there too long, chasing Ash. The man was a ghost in his own time. Now he was Tommy's ghost, chasing him through his dreams, forcing him into a darkness he swore he'd never enter again. Tommy looked at the huge spider web of black and red threads that covered his living space. He was obsessed with finding that connection, with finally catching that demon who'd hunted him and haunted him for a hundred years. He was just as obsessed with catching Maxwell Ash as Ash was with catching him, and they'd both left a trail of dead innocents and ruined lives in their wake.

Tommy didn't care anymore. That's what he knew. The only thing he knew for sure. He had to bury Ash before he could move on. It was more than vengeance. It was his one unfinished job. The one link back to his mortal life that still remained.

He looked at the faces, all those faces on his walls. All those dead men. He hadn't been responsible for that, not directly. But Ash was behind them, and he could have stopped Ash long ago. A split second faster on the trigger, one less moment's hesitation. That's all it would have taken. A little less heart. Ash never would have been able to lead these men to madness and death if Tommy had just pulled the goddamn trigger a half-second sooner.

As he thought, his eyes scanned the room, all those faces, all those ghosts staring back at him.

But there was one who wasn't a ghost. Jared Davis. His picture sat near the door, high up on the wall. Attached to the latest crime. The bank robbery. Where he'd met Allison for the first time. One of those guys was still alive, or at least he was as of yesterday.

Tommy had all the information on him from the police file. What hospital he was in, how heavily he was guarded, everything. Getting into the police computer system hadn't been hard, even for him. He had to talk to this guy before Allison got ahold of him.

Tommy threw his jacket on over his guns. Running down the stairs, he nearly knocked over a neat looking young man who was coming up them. The man gave him a startled look and just stood in the stairwell as Tommy bolted down the steps to the door.

The drive to the hospital took about ten minutes. The emergency room was dealing with minor injuries from Allison's explosive demonstration. There were cops everywhere. Tommy went to the main lobby and looked at the board. Davis was being held in a secure section of the hospital where they treated inmates from the local jail. He was under serious security. Tommy got on the elevator and made his way up to the floor. There were three other departments on this level of the hospital. The neonatal, critical care, and burn ward. Tommy saw the unmarked, secured door to the inmate's wing as soon as he stepped off the elevator. There were two uniformed officers standing outside it. Every time a nurse or doctor went through, they checked IDs and had to push a button on the wall to unlock the door.

Shit. He couldn't just fight his way in. Even if he did get past the cops at the entrance, there were too many hospital personnel around for him to pass unnoticed. He might get into the ward, but they'd catch him long before he'd had a chance to question Davis.

He had to find another way in. These same two cops probably pulled hospital duty on a regular basis. They knew who should be going in and out. Knew them by sight.

Tommy watched the door, doing his best to look inconspicuous in the busy hallway. The cops looked a little bored. One was sipping coffee while the other glanced around the room, occasionally checking the ID badge of a nurse or doctor headed through the door. Sometimes another cop, usually a plainclothes detective, would come to the door. Tommy wondered if they were going in to question the same guy he was, Davis, the bank robber.

Tommy saw several tough looking guys get off the elevator. They were dressed like gang bangers, necks and hands covered in cheap looking prison tattoos. In an inner city hospital, this wasn't anything strange. People from all walks of life wandered in and out of this place. What was strange was the direction they headed: Straight toward the secured wing.

Tommy stepped to the side of the hallway, waiting to see what happened next. He couldn't hear the conversation the gang bangers had with the two cops on guard, but he could tell it was getting heated. Three more guys got off the elevator. They looked similar to the guys who were now arguing with the guards. Different colors, same style. This was about to get ugly.

Tommy heard one of the guys from the newly arrived group yell. The first group turned around to face them. The cops reached for their radios and started frantically calling for backup. As

Tommy watched, the distance between the two groups evaporated as a full blown gang fight erupted in the middle of the hospital.

Nurses and new parents and doctors screamed and dove for cover. Plastic waiting room chairs flew above the crowd like vultures over a kill. Cops and security guards appeared from seemingly every opening in the hallway, including the secured door.

They were coming out of the secured wing. All the cops and security were wading into the gang fight. Tommy saw his chance.

He skirted along the wall of the hallway toward the doorway. The fight was raging now, probably ten to twelve cops and close to twenty gang bangers all going at it in the narrow hall. He got to the door no problem. As he stepped across to press the button, the double doors swung open, and several more police, some plainclothes detectives, came charging through from the secured wing. Tommy had seconds to react. He waited for the cops to pass and slipped between the closing doors behind them.

The hallway was nearly deserted. A couple of nurses wandered from room to room, but for the most part, everybody who might have questioned him being there had gone out to try and break up the fight.

After passing a few doors, he saw the name on a clipboard. *Davis*. Pushing the door open, he saw the bank robber laying there on the hospital bed seemingly hooked up to every monitoring device known to man. The guy had more wires coming out of him than a junction box. Tommy walked over to the bed.

"Davis." He said, leaning toward the man's face. "Davis, wake up!" Tommy shook his shoulder and the sleeping man's eyes popped open.

"I already told the other cops everything I'm gonna say. I want a lawyer. I don't know who did this." Even heavily dosed with morphine, he was a professional. He wouldn't talk to the cops without a lawyer.

"I'm not a cop, Davis."

"Well, you sure as hell ain't a nurse, so get the fuck out of my room." Davis turned his head to the side, facing away from Tommy. He probably would rollover if he could, but he was handcuffed to the bed. Standard procedure with a criminal in a hospital.

"Nope, not a nurse, either." Tommy had to move fast. From in here he had no idea how long it would be before that fight got broken up in the hallway and the guards came back. At most a couple of minutes. He walked down to the end of the bed and looked at the man's chart. "A broken femur, perforated lung, shattered elbow, eight broken ribs, ruptured spleen, broken clavicle, cracked vertebrae, five stab wounds... and a partridge in a pear tree. What did she do, drop you off a building before she shot you?" Tommy chuckled.

"How'd you know it was a woman?" Davis asked, his eyes widening.

"Because I was there, Davis. I know her."

"Oh Jesus Christ! I knew it! I knew somebody would come finish the job!" Davis whimpered.

"Relax, asshole." Tommy said. "I don't honestly care if you live or die at this point. I want information. Give it to me, and I won't kill you."

Davis didn't relax. It doesn't matter how high the dosage, painkillers can't take the fear away. "What information?" He muttered.

"Where's your old P.O.? Where can I find him?"

"I don't want to talk about that, they'll kill me if I do."

Tommy rested his elbow on Davis' broken ribs. The wounded man winced.

"I'll kill you if you don't. But I'll make it *hurt* first." He pressed more weight on the ribs. Davis winced again and then coughed a bit of blood.

"Okay." He whispered. "I'll tell you."

Tommy lifted his weight and let the man breathe. "Tell me where to find him."

"Okay. When he was still my P.O., I used to run errands for him. Simple things. He liked to use his parolees as personal lackeys."

"So?"

"So one night, he calls me drunk, at like three in the morning to take him home from some whore's apartment."

"You know where he lives?"

"Yeah, nice little red house up on Mount Washington. Really clean place. You got a pen? I'll write down the address."

Tommy pulled a notebook out and handed it and a pen to Davis. The man scribbled for a minute before handing it back. Tommy looked at the page. There it was, the address of the one man who could lead him to Ash.

"You're sure this is right?" Tommy asked

"Yeah. He told me to remember that address, because if his wife ever found out where he was that night, that's the address I'd be buried at." Davis said.

"Davis, if this address is wrong, you'll *never* be buried. Because they'll never find you. Understand?" Tommy said, standing straight up at the bedside.

"Yeah. I get it." Davis said in a small, weak voice.

Tommy left the room as Davis turned his head to the window again. They guy was scared. Scared of his employer, scared of Allison, and now scared of Tommy. He'd probably only calm down once they put him in prison for life.

Two guards were walking toward him as Tommy walked back up the hallway. They were talking to each other, both breathing heavily. They barely noticed the guy in the suit walk past them. Probably thought he was a doctor or another detective.

He got to the door and walked back into the lobby. The place was totally wrecked. Furniture broken, the crappy hospital paintings crooked on the walls or laying on the ground ripped. Nurses were crying. There were probably twenty cops in that little lobby, and easily fifteen people in handcuffs sitting in the floor. The rival gang members were still jawing at each other, refusing to give up the fight even now.

Tommy pushed the elevator button. A few of the uniformed officers looked at him sideways as the doors opened and he stepped inside, but he gave them his best *Hey, what can ya do?* look and let the doors close.

As the elevator made its way toward the ground floor, people got on and people got off. Some with the cheery expressions of new parents, others with the peaceful faces of those who'd lost a loved one after a long and painful illness. The hardest faces for him to look into though were the ones who'd obviously lost someone suddenly. Either to illness or tragedy, it didn't matter. Those were the faces Tommy connected with. The sharp, uncontrollable downturn at the corner of the mouth. The agony barely hidden beneath tense musculature. He could tell they were fighting, holding it back. Trying to not show the world their pain. Trying to hide it, to not force it on the other people they crossed paths with on their way to where ever they would be grieving. They fought it back, keeping up appearances for the sake of people they didn't even know.

Tommy understood. How long, after that day in the church in Dublin had he hidden his pain?

How long had he put on a smile or a serious face every day? It was over a hundred years now...

Once he'd gotten off the elevator he checked the notebook again. The address seemed legit. That neighborhood had been there a hundred years ago. He'd gone there a few times in his short stay in Pittsburgh. Back then, it was the area where the better-off working men lived. The middle men of the union and the foremen in the plants. The men who'd actually made it through the ranks somehow, out of the slums and into middle class, ended up on Mount Washington.

Tommy walked out of the lobby and into the crisp air, pulling his overcoat tighter around him. His car was in the parking garage across the street. He looked to both sides before stepping into the road. The streets around hospitals are often the most dangerous places to walk in a city. Not only are ambulances flying everywhere, but people going in and coming out are usually not at their most focused.

As he stepped up onto the sidewalk opposite the hospital, he saw two Paddy wagons pull up near the emergency entrance. A free ride for the gang bangers who had been fighting upstairs. Tommy chuckled to himself and glanced around. He felt that feeling again. He was being watched. He knew the NSA was watching him with their camera feeds, but this felt more personal, more direct. Someone was nearby, watching him from the darkness between the streetlights.

CHAPTER 8

The silver Jag roared out into the snowy city streets. Slush sprayed from the tires as they fought for traction under Tommy's heavy right foot. There was a wide stretch of city and two rivers between him and Mount Washington. It wasn't very far as the crow flies, but in a city built in the mountains, there were no straight lines.

As he slipped and slid through the downtown streets as fast as he dared, Tommy listened to the roar of the six cylinder engine echoing off the silent buildings. Everyone had gone home or gone into one of the local nightspots. Except for the occasional taxi or town car, the streets were dead silent.

The sound reminded him. It reminded him of the roar of machinery, the pumping of engines and steam locomotives. The thunder of coke furnaces spitting sparks into the air as they bubbled, their crucibles of liquid steel and pig iron glowing brightly. Yellow and red in the dim faded light of the soot-stained factories.

It was a sound you had to scream over twenty-four hours a day in those factories. The steel workers got so used to it they developed a form of sign language specific to their jobs. They could explain everything from simple directions such as to where to move the crucible with the gantry to the most intricate details of the recipe for the specific steel they were making. They could make minute adjustments known throughout the factory without ever opening their mouths.

Now he heard that same sound again as his British-made sports car, a luxury that those men on the factory floor couldn't even dream of, shot through the city they built. And *they* built it. That was Tommy's opinion. Not the barons who lived way out in the country and ruled by proxy. Not the government men who decided where the factories and the buildings could go, and who could have the railroad rights. They're not the men who built Pittsburgh. It was those silent, unknown men on the factory floor waving their arms in complex patterns, taking pride in the quality of their work though they were paid next to nothing. The men watching out for the man standing next to them. Those were the men who built this city. The same men built Buffalo and Cleveland. Those men built America.

As he thought about those men he'd met so very many years ago, he careened onto the Smithfield Street Bridge from downtown. There in the gloom and shadow before him loomed Mount Washington. The homes of The Ones Who Made It. Most of the people who lived up here now probably had no idea what kind of people lived in their houses when they were new. Tommy knew for a fact that the dirty Parole Officer he was going to see had no idea of the heritage his home contained.

Now the roads got dangerous. Tommy had to slow down to a near crawl to navigate the steep, twisting streets of this district of the city. He was barely doing thirty miles an hour. The tail of the Jag kept sliding out. It was a common problem with these old cars, but it comes into much clearer focus when the slightest slip will put you through the roof of the house on the street below you.

He finally saw the street sign that would lead him to the Parole Officer's house. Turning right, he pulled up in front a small two-story red house. The yard was well kept, as befitted a man who had some time on his hands and took pride in appearances.

He'd never had a yard, Tommy remembered the last time he'd owned land that wasn't paved. It was a potato farm, and he never really owned it, he paid rent.

As he parked the Jag on the narrow, steep street, Tommy noticed something that made his blood run cold. A black SUV parked up the block. Allison's truck. She was already here.

He jumped out of the car and ran to the door. It was shut, there was no noise coming from inside. He tried the knob. Unlocked. Slowly, he pushed open the door and listened.

There were voices coming from inside. One young, female. One sounded older, a male. There was also a low weeping sound, possibly female. Behind all that, he could hear something else. The cooing of a baby.

Tommy pushed the door open and pulled his guns. Turning to the right he saw the living room. An older man and a woman sat on the couch near the door, huddled together. Gary Collette and his wife. In the opposite corner sat Allison in an ancient looking recliner. A baby, no more than four months old sat peacefully on her lap. One of her hands held the baby upright against her stomach. In the other hand, pointing at the baby's side, was a pistol with a silencer attached.

"Hello, there." Allison said, that fake, psychotic smile spreading across blood red lips. "I was wondering how long it would take you to get here."

Tommy had one gun pointed at the couple, the other at Allison. "How did you find him?"

"Oh, one of the files I stole mentioned him by name. It's not completely decrypted yet, but I got enough. Even though he tried to hide his tracks with an unlisted phone number, home in his wife's maiden name," Allison gestured with the gun to the woman weeping on the couch. "it wasn't hard to find him. They paid him by check. I just followed the money. What about you?"

"Jared Davis. The one guy you *haven't* killed. He was so scared I barely had to touch him." Tommy cocked his pistol. "Put the baby down."

"Heh," Allison looked at the child. "we're just talking. Nothing to worry about. I told them if they didn't let me hold the baby, I'd kill it in its crib. They said yes! Who would have thought?"

"It's amazing what people will do when you point a gun at an infant." Tommy said.

"Isn't it, though?" Allison smiled.

"Go put the baby back in the crib, Allison."

Allison leapt from the chair, leveling her pistol at Tommy. "I don't fucking take orders from you!" She screamed.

"You know that won't kill me." Tommy smiled. "The worst you'll do is piss me off, and I'm halfway there already. I however, won't miss. And this time, I'll shoot you in the fucking head. Now go put the baby back in its crib while I discuss this situation with our friends here."

Allison stared at Tommy. He saw that look on her face. The same look he'd seen the night they first crossed paths. She wanted to kill him, she wanted to kill everybody in the room, at least. But she knew she couldn't kill Tommy. She was going to lose if this came to a fight, and she knew it. Her eyes softened. Not much, but just a little. She lowered her gun and adjusted the baby on her hip.

She turned her back on Tommy and walked toward the stairs that were opposite the front door. As she got to the bottom of the stairs, she turned back to Tommy.

"Don't kill anyone while I'm gone, lover. I wouldn't want to miss anything." She smiled again. That same sick smile. Then she disappeared up the stairs.

Tommy turned to the man and woman still cowering on the couch.

"I don't know who you are or what you want, but thank you." The man blubbered.

"Oh, don't thank me yet, Gary." Tommy said. He swung his left hand at the man, catching him on the forehead with the barrel of his Colt.

The woman screamed. Tommy cocked the pistol in his right hand and pointed it at her.

"Not another sound or you'll never hear that baby's first words, understand?"

The woman nodded. Tommy turned to the man, now laying on the floor holding his head.

"Now, you're going to tell me what you know. Everything you know about Maxwell Ash, The Khlysti, the NSA, and the devices. If I think you're lying, I'll shoot your wife. I won't kill her, but I will *hurt* her. Understand?"

Collette nodded. "Anything you want to know. I'll tell you. Just don't hurt her!"

"Good, then we understand each other."

The man pulled himself to a sitting position on the floor.

Tommy kneeled down in front of the man, pointing one gun at him. "Okay. Tell me everything you know about Maxwell Ash."

"I've never heard that name before. I swear."

"Guy about my height, thin. Possibly a little bit old fashioned. Wears gloves all the time." Tommy said.

"No, I've never seen him. I swear."

Tommy pointed his revolver at the wife's knee.

"I swear I've never seen him or heard that name! The only person I've ever dealt with is Agent Brinson!" Gary said.

"Looks like you have another dead end, Tommy." Allison said from behind him.

"What about The Khlysti?" Tommy asked.

"Are they Russian?" The man responded.

"I met a Russian guy once, he was there with Brinson to show me how one of these gadgets worked. I didn't get a name or anything. He was creepy looking, though. Big thick beard, blue eyes. Scary."

"Rasputin." Allison said.

"Yeah," Collette said. "yeah! He did look a little like Rasputin!"

Tommy stared at the man. "What are they trying to do? What is their plan?"

"I don't know. I swear I don't know. They paid me to find them criminals to use these things, then I never saw the guys again. I figured it was some kind of anti-terror program."

"Why would you think that?" Tommy asked.

"Brinson kept mentioning the possibility of domestic uses. Like spying and such. Plus, isn't that what those NSA guys do?"

"Yeah. That's what they do." Tommy said. He stood up. With his guns in his hands, he towered over the couple like an executioner. "I'm done with you. You're going to go about your life now like nothing ever happened, and forget you ever saw either of us. If you breathe a word of this, we'll come back. Understand?"

Gary Collette and his wife both nodded.

Tommy walked toward the door. Allison walked past him to the couple.

"And," she said. "Just so you don't forget what's at stake." She raised her gun and two quiet puffs went off. The couple screamed almost in unison.

Tommy turned to see them holding their feet. She'd shot them both. He walked out the door and she followed.

Outside, Tommy stopped Allison as she tried to walk to her truck.

"Why the fuck did you do that?" He asked.

"They needed a reminder. Did you think they wouldn't call the police at least after we left?" She responded.

"No, they wouldn't have. Especially after you threatened their grandchild. They would have done everything they could to forget we were ever there!" Tommy said.

"You're making too big a deal of this." Allison said, stepping closer to Tommy. "You're getting all tense about this, and it's really nothing."

Tommy pushed her away. "And you're a fucking nutcase. You're playing way too close to the edge with this. Do you honestly think they won't be able to find you? To stop you? You're not immortal, and you're not a fucking ghost. Eventually, Brinson is going to track you down, and he's not going to arrest you."

"I hope he does!" She said, her voice getting louder. "I hope he does find me. I hope he fucking kills me! I don't belong in this world anymore, and neither do you! One thing's for sure, though. When he does come, I'm taking him out with me!"

"You do what you need to do. I've still got a job to do." Tommy said.

"What, your mystery man? Maxwell Ash, the man who doesn't fucking exist. You think *I've* lost it? The only person who seems to believe that he's even alive is you. And you haven't heard a thing about him in a hundred years. He's dead, Tommy. He's a figment of your twisted imagination. At least what I'm fighting is *real!*" She turned and walked toward her car, leaving Tommy standing on the sidewalk outside the house. As she got to her truck, she turned. "I'll let you know when I have those files decoded. You might find proof that you've lost your mind." She hopped up into the truck and drove off.

As Tommy slid behind the wheel of his car, he felt his phone vibrating in his jacket. The caller ID said Father Daniel. Tommy answered.

"Father, I don't really have time to talk right now." He said.

"I know you don't want to talk to me, Thomas. But you were the only one I thought I could call." Father Daniel replied.

"What's going on, Father?" Tommy said.

"Thomas, I think there are men following me. I don't know who they are, but I've seen them several times over the past few days." He said.

Tommy could hear fear in Father Daniel's voice. "Have they done anything, spoken to you, anything threatening?"

"No, nothing like that. But their presence itself is frightening. They're scary looking guys."

"Okay. If they're not threatening you, just ignore them. They're watching you because of me. Do yourself a favor and don't contact me again until this is all over. You'll be safer that way." Tommy said.

"Oh, Thomas. What have you gotten yourself into?" Father Daniel said.

Tommy heard sirens in the distance. An ambulance and a cop car. "I don't have time to talk about it, Father. I have to go."

Tommy hung up the phone and started the car. The engine roared to life. Slamming it into gear, he pulled away at top speed. He could see the lights of the police car coming over the hill as he navigated the first sharp corner on the hilly streets.

CHAPTER 9

When he finally arrived back at the SRO, he could tell something was different, strange. Usually the place was alive with noise, even at this late hour. There was a never ending din of televisions and yelling. Fights over drugs and relationships that would go on long after midnight. Tonight, nothing. Not a single sound. Tommy locked the door to his room and sat in dark silence. Was Allison right? Could it be that Ash was long dead, and that picture had been put there by someone else? Who would have done that? Brinson? Was it possible that he'd done it to throw Tommy off? To make him chase ghosts instead of the real sources of what was going on?

Tommy didn't think so, but the evidence was stacking in that direction. There was no way even Ash was so good that he could build such a collection of devices, get involved so deep in a government program, and still not leave a single trace of himself behind. Tommy hadn't done it, and he'd purposely avoided contact with anyone or anything that could have tracked him. Yet they still knew about him. They knew every detail of his life going back a hundred years.

He looked around at the detritus that had become his life. Papers strewn about the room. Piles of this and that stacked everywhere there could be a stack that wouldn't fall over. Empty food containers piled that should have been taken to the trash months ago now have sat so long that even the flies had given up on them. What was this? Was this where the story lead? Was this the final outcome of his hundred year search for absolution?

A faint sound in the hall pulled him out of his thoughts. Quiet footsteps. A hint of noise in the unnaturally silent hall. A sound of metal against metal. A door lock? Someone chambering a round into an MP5? What was that sound? Static from outside the door. Radio static or someone's television going off air from a local channel?

Tommy stood up and turned. There was a tiny reflection under the door. A small black tube with a lens on the end. A lipstick camera.

He turned and grabbed the desk full of papers. In one swift motion he'd pulled it away from the wall and dumped it on its side between the window and the door. He ducked down behind it and pulled his pistols out.

Moments later the door exploded in. There was aggressive yelling and a loud bang and blinding light of a flash grenade. He raised his head over the heavy wood desk and saw a man in black riot gear and a gas mask coming into the room. Tommy fired a shot over the desk, hitting the man in the shoulder. The man fell in place. Two other men fired blind into the room as they pulled the wounded man back out into the hall.

There were at least three. One mostly down. Two left. Tommy cocked both his pistols and waited for them to storm the room. An arm appeared in the doorway. Tommy fired into the hall, but missed the arm. Something got lobbed his way, bouncing off the wall and landing a couple feet away from him.

Tommy glanced at it. Cylindrical. Grey. Small. Smoking. Grenade. He tried to dive out of the way. The world around him exploded in a shower of white. A high pitched ringing filled his head. He was blinded, deaf. There were murmurs of noise. His eyes burned. Vague thoughts of being handcuffed, dragged. Struggling. A sharp pain in his head. Silence.

Dark blurs filled his reconstituting vision. He was seated. His hands were bound to the chair. He shook his head, trying to get his vision clear.

"A bit groggy still, Mr. McKinney?" A familiar voice said. "Give it a bit of time. You'll come around. You were struggling so much my men felt the need to knock you out. Of course, they didn't feel too bad about it, you did shoot Johnson."

"Johnson should know better than to be first through the door, Brinson." Tommy said. As he spoke, the thin man in the tailored suit came into focus, sitting in a chair opposite him. Two large men stood on either side of him holding MP5s.

"I could send you to prison for attempted murder of a federal agent. You know that, right?" Brinson said.

"Yeah, but you won't. I have a feeling the last thing you want is a public trial showing the world what you're actually doing." Tommy replied.

"That is a concern." Said Brinson. "However, being that you associate with known terrorists, I doubt there'd be a public trial. Straight to Guantanamo Bay for you."

"Heh. Terrorist. Interesting term. I wonder what they'd call you? Experimenting on soldiers, torturing women and babies." Tommy said.

"One day they'll call me a hero for saving this country and the world. That's what they'll call me." Brinson leaned forward in his chair. "But they won't call you anything."

"Why's that?" Tommy asked.

"You think you're immortal, don't you? You've survived drowning, shootings, torture. A hundred and forty three years. But I don't think you're immortal, Mr. McKinney. The way I see it, if I take off your head, you'll stop. If I pump enough bullets into you, even that fast healing trick you pull wouldn't be able to restart your heart. And as I know you're fully aware, dead is dead." The tone in Brinson's voice was disturbing. He was speaking as though he had first hand knowledge of this.

"Anything's possible, Brinson." Tommy said.

"I know you're working with Allison." Brinson stood up from the chair as he spoke. "I also know that you're looking for something that can cure your so-called curse. You have been for years. We know all about you, you've been on our radar for decades."

"I kinda figured that." Tommy said. "My question is this: How did Maxwell Ash, who's lived just as long as I have, stay off your radar for so long?"

"If I were you, Mr. McKinney, I'd stop looking for Maxwell Ash. You're not going to find him. You should be worrying about yourself now." Brinson said.

"Oh, should I? Maybe you're the one who should be worried. Worried about that pretty book you've been looking for, Merrick's Codex?" Tommy asked, his lips twisting into an arrogant grin.

Agent Brinson's body tightened. His hands clenched into fists. He leaned in to Tommy, just inches from his face. "What do you know about the Codex?" He asked.

"I know it contains everything Merrick knew about the devices, everything he'd learned from studying the centuries of watchmakers. I know it is a *very* powerful book." Tommy smiled, looking over Brinson's now shaking form standing over him. "I also know," he said, "that you have no idea where it is."

"That book," Brinson whispered, "contains very important information. Information about a weapon so powerful that knowledge of it could change the balance of power in the world. If you know anything about its whereabouts at all, tell me now and it might just be the thing that saves your life. Refuse to tell me what you know and," Brinson pulled a folding knife out of his pocket and opened it, "we'll get it out of you anyway."

"You know," Tommy said, "I was tortured once. By a Nazi. They guy was good. Tortured me for *months*. He knew every pressure point, every way to make a man hurt and believe that the hurting would never stop. He was very, very good at his job."

"So?" Brinson asked.

"So, one day, this Nazi takes me in to the torture room and starts up his little routine. Pulling out the blades, showing them to me one by one, telling me exactly what he's going to do to me with them. The whole deal." Tommy says.

"What are you getting at?" Asked Brinson.

"Well," Tommy said, "That day, I decided he was done. I killed fourteen other men, tortured that Nazi for a half an hour with his own tools, accomplished my mission, and walked happily back into my country, never having divulged a word.

What makes you think that your little pocket knife scares me at all?"

Brinson tried to stare into Tommy's eyes, tried to out man him. It wasn't going to happen. Tommy saw that Nazi bastard. He saw the British soldiers who'd spent hours dowsing him with cold water, beating him, making him sleep in his own piss and shit. This little government troll wasn't going to have the best of him. Not today.

There was sudden noise from outside the room. Gunfire, screaming. The two guards' radios crackled to life. There was shouting coming out of them. Brinson straightened himself up as one of the guards leaned down to speak into his ear. He motioned to the guards to go help. They left the room cocking their MP5s.

"It seems as though we didn't need you to find Allison. She's come to *us*." Brinson said, smiling slightly.

Tommy's arrogant grin got wider.

"What are you smiling at?" Brinson screamed.

"If she's come here," Tommy said, "You're in big, big trouble."

Tommy flew forward as steel door to the detainment room flew past him. He could hear sporadic gunfire in the hallway beyond, the sounds of men screaming, then silence. When he opened his eyes, he couldn't see Brinson anymore. Face down, still attached to the now mangled chair, his field of view was limited, but the room seemed empty. He felt a gloved hand on his wrist. He struggled to get away as he felt a blade slide against the bare flesh of his forearm.

"Don't struggle, lover," Allison whispered in his ear, "I'm trying to cut you free."

Tommy stopped fighting. Within seconds the bonds on his hands and legs were cut. As he stood up, Allison threw him his pistols, still in the holsters.

"Where did you get these?" He asked.

"The guards in the next room stopped struggling after I killed them." She said, a wild look in her eye.

She was loving this, loving every bloody second of it.

"Come on," she said, "I doubt I killed them all on the way down, and they've probably got reinforcements by now."

Tommy checked his guns. They were still loaded, but he was three bullets short in one. Only nine shots left total, and no spare ammo. Tommy looked around, and saw Brinson's knife on the floor. He picked it up and examined its four inch blade.

"That should do." He said, turning his head toward the hole where the door used to be.

Allison led the way out into the hall. Tommy followed close behind. He kept his pistols in their holsters, holding the folding knife open in his left hand. They moved to the end of the hall, Allison holding the barrel of her M16 just ahead of Tommy.

The hallway ended in a T intersection. A man in riot gear stepped around the corner just as Tommy reached it. Without hesitating, Tommy jabbed the short blade of the knife into the man's throat. He dropped to the floor with one hand at his neck, trying to stem the flow arterial blood.

Another guard was within reach as Tommy rounded the corner in the direction the guard had come from. He grabbed the barrel of the guard's gun with his right hand, spinning him around. Two more guards who were coming up the hall stopped in their tracks as Tommy held the bloody knife to the guard's throat.

Before he could tell them to drop their guns, Allison opened fire. She sprayed the men with bullets until they dropped on the floor, the machine gun fire filled the narrow hall with a brutal roar that rang in his ears. It didn't help that the barrel was just inches from his head.

"Was that necessary? He asked.

"What," Allison looked up at him smiling, "and let you have *all* the fun?"

Tommy pushed the guard down the hall toward the door at the end. He saw a flight of stairs through the small window. They didn't lead down, only up.

"We're on the ground floor?" He asked Allison.

"No, sweetie," she said, "we're in the fourth sub-basement."

"Up, then?" He said.

"Up. Two floors." She said. "I have a plan."

"Great." Tommy said. He grabbed the guard by either side of his head and twisted. The man's neck broke with a sick, wet sounding crunch.

"Don't need him anymore." He said.

"I do love watching you work." Allison said, her eyes bright as she stared down at the dead guard's face, now turned the wrong way on his body.

Tommy opened the door to the stairwell. He could hear boots on the stairs several floors above, coming down. Once they got past the next level up, they could be caught in a vertical crossfire. Not good.

"What's your plan in case they flank us?" He asked.

"Oh," Allison smiled and adjusted her backpack straps, "I have a plan for that, too. Now just go."

Tommy started up the stairwell taking two steps at a time. He hoped he'd get to sub-basement two before the next wave of guards. He had an advantage: It was easier to run *up* than it was to run *down*. On top of that, they had to worry about tripping up the men behind and in front of them. He had a feeling he didn't have to worry about Allison tripping at all.

As they reached the landing for Sub Level Three, Allison stopped behind Tommy. He was already starting up the next set of stairs by the time he realized she wasn't behind him. He turned to see her kneeling over her bag with her rifle on the floor. She looked up at him, picking up the weapon.

"Mind holding this for a minute? I have to do something." She said.

Tommy took the gun from her hand and looked up the stairwell. He could still hear the boots coming down the stairwell, but they seemed a good ways off. He glanced back at Allison and saw her press five small grey blocks against the frame of the door, each about the size of a chocolate bar. C4, and a lot of it. She carefully pressed a silver detonator into each of the blocks and ran the detonator wire to another small piece of C4 near the handle of the door.

"Don't you think that's a bit much?" Tommy asked.

"Depends on what you're trying to achieve." Allison said, smiling.

She pressed a small black box against the wall next to the door, stretching a thin wire tightly across the gap. She pressed another little metal box against the door and attached the wire. After this was done, Allison stood up and glanced through the small window in the door.

"Can't have anyone coming through until we're clear." She said, kneeling back down.

Tommy looked up the stairwell. The boots were getting closer. He didn't think they were on the next landing yet, but it wouldn't be long.

Allison plugged the detonator wires into the small black box on the door. She stood up and walked past Tommy, taking the rifle from him.

"Come on," she said, "if they come through that door now, the blast will kill us, too."

Tommy followed her up the stairs. She was taking them two at a time, and Tommy was having trouble keeping up. He realized his ears were still ringing from the flash bang grenade in his room. He felt unsteady on his feet, couldn't seem to get his vision to clear. The whole world seemed just out of focus. He thought he might have a concussion from the blast.

As Allison reached the Sub Level Two landing, gunfire ripped through the tile at her feet. She jumped back just in time to dodge the second volley from the men on the landing above them. She slid back down the steps to Tommy, who had stopped halfway up the stairs.

"If we're going to get out of this building," she said, "we have to get through that door." She pointed at the door to Sub Level Three just above them.

"How many men?" Tommy asked, sliding the knife into his pocket and pulling out his guns.

"Five that I could see," she said, aiming her rifle at the landing above them, "they're on the landing between Levels Two and One."

Tommy looked at the stairs. They were pretty standard for an office building. Reinforced concrete. No handholds underneath. He couldn't see a way to get behind the guards. Allison was moving, and it caught Tommy's attention. He saw her reach into her backpack and pull out a round, green object about the size of a baseball. Grenade. He grabbed her arm as she reached for the pin.

"What are you doing?" She hissed. "Don't ever touch me."

Tommy let go of her arm. "You try to throw that from here, you'll miss. Best case it brings the whole fucking staircase down on us. Worst case, it hits the wall and bounces down, setting off your C4. Either way, we're still fucked!"

"We're fucked right now!" Allison said.

"Maybe not. Let me think. Anybody comes down that stairwell, shoot to disable. A hostage might be handy." Tommy said.

Tommy leaned against the wall. He'd been here before. Baton Rouge. With Beaux. Then he was dealing with a bunch of semi-trained weekend warriors. The men above him now were professional. Every single one a trained killer.

Even having a hostage might not keep them from shooting at this point. Especially if they had heard what he did to the guy downstairs.

Tommy stopped. He listened. No one was moving. They were holding position. Only two reasons for that. Either they were waiting for orders, or reinforcements. No way they were waiting for orders, not now. They were waiting for more men. Brinson only needed him to get to Allison. She was right here. No reason to keep either of them alive now.

There was no way out. Tommy could see that. In a few seconds, guards would come bursting through the door for Sub Level Three. The door right below them. Allison had wired close to four pounds of C4 to that door. When it blew, it would take out everything within two hundred feet, including them, the guards above them, and pretty much the entire stairwell.

No more time to think. Tommy cocked his pistols and ran up the stairs to the landing. The guards didn't expect it. Their first shots hit the ground at his feet. He managed to take out two of the guards before one of the remaining got his aim in. A round hit Tommy in the thigh, dropping him to his knee. They were good, well trained. He was better. As he dropped he re-cocked his guns. He took another round in the right shoulder as he fired. It threw off his aim a bit, sending the bullet into the guard's arm instead of his chest, above the bulletproof vest.

Tommy felt a hand on his collar. Allison slammed the door to Sub Level Two open and pulled him through on his back. She slammed the door shut behind them. Stopping for a moment, she threw Tommy's arm over her shoulder and helped him to his feet, taking part of his weight as they made their way down the hall. Tommy tried not to wince as she pulled on his newest bullet wound.

"What the hell were you thinking? Do you have a death wish?" Allison hissed.

"You read their file on me. You should know it's my *greatest* wish." Tommy hissed back.

A huge blast rocked the hall behind them. Tommy turned just in time to see the steel door into the stairwell lodge itself in the ceiling. A light red mist that he assumed was the remains of the guards in the stairwell floated in the air.

Allison followed Tommy's gaze.

"I love a foggy night too," she said, "but right now, I have work to do. We're not going to have this hall to ourselves for long." She leaned Tommy against the wall and handed him her M16.

"Cover me." She said.

Tommy stood between her and the end of the hallway that hadn't just been blown straight to Hell. He raised the rifle to his shoulder and blinked, trying to get the haze in his vision to clear. Something was there, something between the world and his eyes, but he couldn't seem to pierce it. At short distances like the stairwell, it wasn't an issue. Out here, aiming down a hundred yard long hall, it could make a big difference. There was nowhere to hide if shooting started. He and Allison would be exposed to aimed fire. If someone popped out at the end of the hall, he had to be accurate.

What was that haze? It wasn't from the flashbang, he'd dealt with those before. It was something else, something almost not physical. It was like he was wearing dirty sunglasses he couldn't take off.

As Tommy watched, the floor in the hall changed. It seemed to vibrate for a moment. Turning liquid and draining away to expose unpolished stone underneath. Tommy shook his head. The tile floor returned for a moment then faded back out to stone. He knew that floor. He knew the hallway. He'd seen it before, but where? Wooden doors lined it now, set into stone walls. A dim light from bare bulbs in metal fixtures glinted off the frosted glass set into the doors.

He recognized it now. The hallway, the lights, the stone floor. It was Austria, the prison.

This hallway led to the torture cell. These were administrative offices for the SS officers stationed there. He could hear the faint beep of Morse Code coming from down the hallway.

No. It wasn't. It wasn't World War Two. It was two thousand thirteen. He was in the basement of an NSA office. He had to focus.

Tommy closed his eyes. He shook his head violently, his hair falling across his forehead. When he opened his eyes again, the old hallway was gone. The hallucination was over, replaced by the stark polished linoleum tile and plain white walls of a modern office building. He turned his head. Allison was taping what looked like string to the wall. Thick, orange string.

"What are you doing?" He asked, looking back down the hall.

"Detcord." She responded. "This wall runs parallel to the city's storm drains. You might want to move a little further down the hall." She put her hand in Tommy's lower back and guided him down the hall. His bloody shoulder left a streak of red along the wall. Tommy looked down and was a small pool of blood forming at his left foot.

The blast from the detcord shook the wall he was leaning on, sending spikes of pain through his shoulder. Allison took the M16 from him and threw his arm over her shoulder. They made their way from the well-lit hallway into the darkness of the storm drain.

"The government may own the streets, but these tunnels are mine." Allison said.

They moved through the tunnels as fast as Tommy's leg would allow. Allison had them memorized. She made turns without having to check a map or even really think about it. About three hundred yards in, she stopped.

"Do you hear that?" She said, leaning Tommy against the wall and stepping a few feet back down the tunnel.

Tommy strained his ears. There was a noise, thought he had no idea how Allison had heard it over the noise of their own feet moving through the mucky runoff of the city. Splashing. Lots of splashing. Feet moving through the tunnels.

"They're coming." Allison hissed.

"Don't know how they found us, not like we left a big-ass hole in the wall." Tommy said.

"Did you have a better idea?" She said.

"I'm still not sure why you went in there at all." He said.

"Time for that later. Right now," Allison said, throwing Tommy's arm over her shoulder again, "we have to get further down the tunnel if we're going to have any chance of defending ourselves. We can't outrun them with your leg like that."

She led Tommy further into the maze. Every hundred yards or so they passed through a junction. Sometimes turning left, sometimes right. For the most part they were traveling in a straight line.

After several minutes, they reached a large junction point with nine tunnels coming off it. Allison again leaned Tommy against the wall. She walked around the fifteen foot diameter round room, shutting and bolting the steel doors at the end of the tunnels leading in except two. One was the tunnel they had just come through, and another just a few feet from it.

"We'll take some of them here." She said, checking her M16. "At least we'll be able to thin their numbers."

"How many men do you think they sent into these tunnels?" Tommy asked.

"Oh, my guess is most of them," Allison smiled at Tommy, "These guys don't fuck around."

Tommy checked his own guns. Four and two.

"I don't suppose you have any .45 Long Colt rounds in that little bag of tricks?" He asked.

"Nope," she said, "but I do have these." She pulled two 9mm Glocks out of the bag with an extra clip for each.

Tommy holstered his revolvers and took the pistols from Allison, checking that there were rounds chambered in each.

Allison walked over to the tunnel and shot out the overhead light in the tunnel. Then she turned and shot out the light above them, leaving only the dim glow from the manhole cover above them to light the room. The noise reverberated around the circular room.

"They'll be using night vision, I'll bet my life on it." She said into the darkness.

"Then what good is shooting out the lights?" Tommy hissed.

"Just wait." She said.

Tommy's eyes adjusted enough to let him get his bearings. He slid along the wall to a point that gave him a decent view of the incoming tunnel. He stood there waiting.

Allison was not far away, covering the tunnel from Tommy's right. She was kneeling against the wall with her rifle hanging at her side and something in her hand. Another grenade?

Tommy didn't have time to think about what she was going to do. He heard voices and footsteps coming from the tunnel. The men had tracked them from the last junction and were closing in. The voices and footsteps got louder and louder. He waited to see what she'd do. They were moving cautiously. Tommy figured they'd be stepping out of the tunnel at any moment.

Allison moved. Tommy saw her hands move first, then a second or two passed. She lobbed something into the tunnel just as Tommy saw a foot cross the threshold of the tunnel. The foot disappeared back down the tunnel.

"Ears!" Allison screamed.

Tommy got his hands over his ears just as the flashbang went off. He could hear the men in the tunnel screaming. She'd blown out their ears and blinded them with their own night vision. Tommy leaned off the wall, looking down the tunnel. Three men were laying on the round, another two were trying to pull them to safety. He opened fire the same time as Allison.

They sprayed the tunnel with lead. The two men who were still standing dropped first, then they turned on the incapacitated men on the ground. Allison emptied a clip into their writhing bodies.

Tommy looked at her in the dim light. She was laughing.

Gunfire tore through the wall behind them. Reinforcements. Allison threw another flashbang down the tunnel. Tommy covered his ears as she slammed the tunnel door shut. The roar was still almost deafening.

"Time to go." Tommy said.

Allison was already moving toward the escape tunnel.

"That door won't hold them for long." She said. "They can be opened from both sides."

She helped Tommy into the escape tunnel and turned to shut the door behind them. Now he saw why she took the time to shut the other tunnel doors: Once the guards got into the junction room, they'd have to figure out which tunnel Tommy and Allison had left through.

They made their way further into the labyrinth of tunnels under the city. Tommy had no idea where they were now. Allison had taken a good bit of his weight the entire walk. He figured that she had above average stamina, but her ability to keep going was tremendous.

They passed junction after junction, moving as fast as his wounded leg would carry him. He was losing a lot of blood. It had soaked through his clothes and he could feel it pooling in his shoe, mixing with the trash filled water of the city's runoff.

When they had reached yet another junction point, Allison stopped. Letting go of Tommy, she looked around.

"They're probably pretty close again by now." She said. "We're under the south side of the city." Her eyes focused on the ceiling of the tunnel, moving part way around the room then stopping, over and over again until she had made a full circuit.

Tommy followed her eyes. He saw wires running along the roof of the room. They were dirty and almost blended into the grimy walls. The wires ran between five small rectangles set evenly spaced around the room near the ceiling.

Allison helped Tommy into yet another tunnel. She went over to the wall and pulled out a pair of wires that had been hidden in gaps in the stonework. To these she hooked a transmitter, flicking a switch on the back. Pulling a small remote from her bag, she walked back to where Tommy was standing in the tunnel and shut the door, locking it.

"Now," she said, "we wait."

Tommy realized her plan. She was going to wait until the guards had gone into the junction and then bring the whole tunnel down on them, leaving them dead and anyone who came in behind them with no idea where he and Allison had gone. This was where she ended the trail.

She must have set this up months ago, at least. It was part of her escape route. They were headed for her safe house.

They sat there in the tunnel for what seemed like minutes. Allison had backed them off about a hundred feet in case the door got blown out. She was like a statue, standing perfectly still, listening.

Tommy was fighting to focus now. If he could stem the flow of blood, he'd feel fine in a couple of hours. It would take days for the bullet wounds to heal, but the blood he'd lost would come back quickly. He still had the 9mm pistols in his hands. The right one was dripping his blood.

So much blood, decades of it now. Tommy looked down in the dim light of the tunnel and saw his blood mixing with the water. Dripping off the barrel of a gun to blend with the rest of the refuse of the city. Was that what he'd become? A part of the trash?

Voices in the distance pulled him back. Allison had tensed. She had her finger on the button. One voice, then two, then four. They became clearer as the men entered the junction room.

She pushed the button. The whole tunnel shook. Chunks of the ceiling over their heads dropped on them, leaving Tommy covered in moss and wet grime. The solid steel door to their tunnel didn't blow off, but Tommy saw it warp. He wondered what kind of chaos was on the other side of that door now.

Allison took his arm and started leading him further down the tunnel.

"Now we really have to move." She said. "That blast was designed to cave in the street. There's going to be all sorts of people we don't want to see in these tunnels in a minute."

She led him through another quarter mile of tunnels, stopping occasionally to listen for footsteps. There weren't any. Her plan seemed to have worked.

Finally she stopped at a junction. Climbing the ladder to the manhole, she pressed her ear against the cold metal and listened. Apparently satisfied, she pushed the heavy cover aside, climbing through.

CHAPTER 10

Tommy fought his way up the ladder with one arm and one leg. It took him a few minutes, but soon Allison was pulling him by his good arm into a dark corner of the warehouse she called home.

Allison dragged him over to the bed before disappearing again. She returned moments later with a stainless steel tray holding forceps, a needle and thread, a large bowl of water, and gauze.

"I'm guessing you can do the next part yourself?" She asked, smiling.

"Most likely." Tommy said. He sat up and fought through the head rush.

"When you're done, come over here. You'll want to see this." She said.

Allison set the tray down next to him and closed the divider between the sleeping area and the rest of her "home". Tommy set to work.

They had used hollow point bullets. Pretty standard for police and government issue. There was a lot of damage. Tommy fought his leg out of his pants and looked and the hole in his thigh. It was just above the knee, didn't look like it hit anything major. If it had punctured his femoral artery, he'd have at least passed out from blood loss long ago.

As he dug around in his leg for the bullet, He thought about what Brinson had said. Could he be killed? Was it possible that he could die just like anyone else? He'd always wondered. Brinson sounded so *sure*.

He felt the forceps click. He'd found the bullet in his thigh muscle. It was deep. Another inch or so and it would have torn a grapefruit-sized hole in the back of his leg. As it was, it had torn through plenty of muscle, ripped arteries and veins apart.

Tommy gritted his teeth and squeezed the bullet. Holding on to the steel bed frame, he pulled with steady tension, dragging the deformed mass of lead across raw nerves and inflamed tissue until finally it broke the surface. He looked at it in the fluorescent light. Another bullet. One of God knows how many he's pulled out or left in.

He dropped the round onto the concrete at his feet. Picking up the needle and thread, he once again gritted his teeth and sewed together the Quarter-sized hole in his thigh before wiping it clean with the water and cloth.

He was winded. He took long, slow, deep breaths. This wasn't his safe house, and the fight wasn't over yet. He couldn't afford to black out this time, and there was still another bullet wound to deal with.

He pulled off his jacket and peeled himself out of his blood soaked white dress shirt and shoulder holsters. This one wasn't as deep. As far as straight shots went, it wasn't much more than a flesh wound. The bullet had hit him just outside the clavicle, slamming into the top of the humerus. It had probably broken the bone, but that would heal if it got the chance. He dug the forceps into his shoulder, trying to get it over with as quickly as possible. But this bullet was being a pain in the ass.

Hitting the bone made it fragment. Tommy pulled out six small pieces that didn't add up to a whole bullet before deciding to leave the rest in place. He rotated his shoulder a few times, nearly screaming in pain, just to make sure none of the remaining bits of lead impeded his range of motion. Finally satisfied, he fought through sewing up the still bleeding wound and pressed a piece of self-adhesive gauze to it.

Once he was done with his shoulder, he pressed gauze against the stitches on his leg and wrapped his thigh with another strip to hold it in place.

Tommy didn't want to put those bloody clothes back on. They were soaked through. He wrapped himself in Allison's blanket and walked around the divider into the area where she was sitting.

"Getting my blanket all bloody?" She asked.

"No point in putting those clothes back on." He responded.

She made a disgusted face and turned to the computer.

"You should see this." She said, pointing to the screen. "These are the files I got from our little foray into the NSA offices the other night."

Tommy looked at the screen. There were several files open. The top one was what looked like a final operational report. He scanned the page as best as his blurry eyes could. Something about tracking the subject. Years and years of tracking the subject. Buffalo, then out west somewhere in Arizona for a few years. It went on and on. Decades. Tommy thought it looked familiar. He was in Buffalo, same time. He went to Arizona, but he left for San Francisco a few months before whoever this was.

Someone had been following him since the beginning. Since all this madness started. Tommy scrolled down to the bottom of the page. Buffalo again, right after the Katrina incident. Then Baton Rouge. There was a note in parentheses after that notation.

Subject B seems to be attempting to force a confrontation with Subject A. He has intentionally made himself visible at a distance to Subject A against explicit orders to stay clear. Subject B has intentions of drawing Subject A to Pittsburgh, the city of their first meeting, in order to eliminate Subject A. Subject B's assistance is no longer mission critical due to recent development of relationship with Subject C. Recommend immediate removal of Subject B from project. All care should be taken to keep Subject A ignorant of removal of Subject B. Subject A could be instrumental in the capture of "Allison".

Tommy couldn't believe what he was reading. It was Ash. He was there. He was in Buffalo. He was in Baton Rouge. He was working with the NSA. Tommy had to be Subject A, then, and he had a pretty damned good idea who Subject C was. It had to be Rasputin.

He scanned further. There were more notes about Ash, he travelled up the east coast. He beat Tommy to Pittsburgh by just a few days. At the end of the page there was a final parenthetical notation, dated two days before Tommy got to Pittsburgh.

Subject B removed from program. Eliminated. Confirmed.

-Brinson

Ash was dead. Confirmed dead. These guys knew what he was, how hard it was to kill a man like Ash or Tommy. If they confirmed it, they meant it. That's why Brinson sounded so confident when he said Tommy could die. He'd killed Maxwell Ash.

Ash was dead. Tommy had been chasing a ghost for months. Everyone had been right, at least partially. Ash had been in Baton Rouge and Buffalo. Tommy wasn't hallucinating, not about that.

Allison's voice pulled Tommy out of his train of thought.

"There's something else you need to see," she said, clicking the mouse a couple of times, "I just decoded these yesterday. They're the reason I broke you out."

A file opened up. There was a picture of a young, tough looking man at the top right. Underneath was the name *Michael "Beaux" Lafontaine*. They had a file on Beaux.

It recounted his full involvement in the Baton Rouge incident, but it went further. Beaux's father was listed as a known *device using* career criminal. He'd died in prison two years after Beaux was born.

Attached to the end of the file was a capture notice with an action date listed as two days ago. He was wanted for study and interrogation. Tommy needed his coat. He needed to get his phone to warn Beaux. Allison stopped him.

"Before you do anything," she said, "you need to see this." She clicked the mouse again. Another file opened.

He saw the picture. He didn't need to read the file. He jumped straight to the bottom of the page. An interview order, action date of two days ago. A kill order, action date today. They were going to kill Father Daniel.

Tommy limped over to his coat. He dialed the number for Father Daniel's office. It rang several times before someone picked up.

"Hello?" An elderly female voice said.

"I need to speak to Father Daniel. It's an emergency." Tommy almost yelled into the phone.

"Calm down, dear. What's the emergency?" The woman said.

"This is Tommy McKinney. I need to speak with Father Daniel immediately." Tommy said.

"Oh, Mr. McKinney. Father's spoken of you. My name is Sister Marguerite. I'm Father Daniel's office aide. In fact, just the other day there were some men here asking him about you." She said.

"Do you know what he told them? Sister, it's very important." Tommy said.

"He told them he didn't know you. I don't know why he lied to them, but he told me that if they asked me, I should tell them the same thing. He said it was a Papal Order. I don't like lying, but if the Holy Father says I need to protect someone, I'll do what he says, you know." Sister Marguerite said.

"That's very good, Sister. Where is Father Daniel now?" Tommy asked.

"Oh, he's out in the cemetery. He likes to care for the graves himself when he can. You know he's not a young man anymore." Sister Marguerite said.

"Sister," Tommy said as calmly as he could, "you need to get him back into the church. You need to do that for me, tell him I'm coming. His life is in danger."

"Oh, he knows that, dear. Have a safe trip." Sister Marguerite hung up the phone.

Tommy stared at the phone for a moment. What the hell did that mean? Nuns. He shook his head and started dialing again.

"Who are you calling now?" Allison asked.

"Beaux." Tommy said, listening to the phone ring. "I have to warn him that they're coming."

Tommy heard noise come through the phone.

"Hello?" said a muffled voice. It was difficult to understand through the roar in the background.

"Beaux?" Tommy said.

"Yeah. This is Beaux." Said the voice.

"Beaux, it's Tommy. Where the hell are you?" Tommy said.

"Just outside Harrisburg, Pennsylvania. I'm on my bike. What do you need, Tommy?" Beaux said.

"Beaux, the NSA is coming after you. They're coming after Father Daniel." Tommy said.

"I know. They tried to get me a couple days ago. They didn't know who they were dealing with. I'm headed to Buffalo now. Where are you?" Beaux said.

"I'm in Pittsburgh. They're after me, too." Tommy said.

"I figured if they were after me, they'd be after you. Since I hadn't heard from you, I figured they'd already gotten you." Beaux said.

"They already did, twice. Listen, I'm going to Buffalo. I have to protect Father Daniel." Tommy said.

"I had the same thought. I'm a little over four hours away." Beaux said.

"I'll meet you there." Said Tommy.

Tommy hung up the phone. He stared at the floor. How had everything gotten so twisted? A simple priest and a relative kid from Baton Rouge wrapped up in a government plot? He couldn't let it happen. He couldn't let anything happen to them.

"I'm going to Buffalo." He said.

"I figured you were." Allison said.

"I can't go back to my room. I need you to take me to my car. I have clothes there, and ammunition." Tommy said.

"I can do that. Who do you think is in Buffalo? Is it Brinson?" She asked.

"Brinson, Rasputin, maybe both. There's no way to know, but someone is questioning Father Daniel. We might both find our answers in Buffalo." Tommy said.

"I'm going with you." Allison said, standing. "If either of them are there, I'll make them pay for what they did to me."

"Okay, but I still need my car." Tommy said.

"We can get clothes and ammo." She said.

"No, I need my *car.*" He responded. "Call it sentimentality."

Allison shrugged. "Whatever." She said.

"Now," Tommy said, wrapping the blanket around himself and picking up his shoulder holsters, "take me to my Jag."

Allison drove like a maniac getting to the underground parking lot where Tommy had left his Jag. She stood there watching as he stripped down nude and put on the fresh suit he kept in the trunk.

"Not bad." She said, smiling.

Tommy reloaded his Peacemakers and slid them into their holsters. "Try and keep up." He said.

He hobbled over to the driver's door of the Jag and slid in. Starting the engine, he sat listening to it for several seconds. That roar, that thunderous roar bouncing off the concrete walls of the parking garage. He loved that sound, always had.

Once the car had settled into a low idle he dropped it into gear, roaring out of the garage at top speed with Allison close behind in her SUV.

CHAPTER 11

Once he was on the highway, Tommy had time to think. They were driving blind into something, possibly something huge, and most likely had the entire NSA looking for them. For a hundred years he'd stayed low. Mostly out of trouble, mostly out of sight. He'd taken things as they came, always waiting for the day he could square his sins with God and have this curse of immortality taken off him.

Was that really what he'd been trying to do? He'd killed people. At this point, probably hundreds of them. He couldn't even remember anymore. There were so many nightmares in the shadows, so many demons just out of sight. Was his life just the culmination of all those demons and secrets now? He was a dangerous man; he'd known that for a very long time. But he'd always thought that he was only dangerous to bad people.

All this, though. All this made him rethink that. How many innocents had been hurt because of him? Katrina, Scotty, now Beaux and Father Daniel. How many others had there been that he didn't remember, or didn't even know about? He was a wrecking ball. He wasn't a surgical tool. He was no better than the men he hunted: Driven, mad, and dangerous to anyone he came into contact with.

Tommy let his mind wander through the centuries. It was a long road from Pittsburgh to Buffalo, but a longer, broken road from where he started to where he was.

It started in Ireland. So very, very long ago. He was good then, normal then. He had a future, a family. He was alive. Then it all came apart. He hadn't noticed it, hadn't seen how far he'd slipped until it was too late. It was after Pittsburgh, after his first run in with Ash. It was the First World War.

He'd joined up with the Canadians. They entered the war before the U.S. He told himself that he wanted to protect people, to fight for the right side. Somewhere inside he knew, though. He knew the real reason he'd joined was that he'd wanted to kill. As many people as possible. He was trying to quench the rage, the hate inside. But no matter how many Germans he killed, no matter how much blood he spilled in the fields of France, he could never wash the blood of his wife and child off his hands. They hadn't died at his hand, but they might as well have. He always felt like he should have done more, that he could have saved them.

They gave him medals. Lots of medals. They said he was a hero. He wasn't a hero. He was a murderer. He didn't kill for his country. He didn't kill to protect his comrades in the trenches. He killed because he enjoyed it. Simple as that. There was no other reason.

After the Armistice, he stayed in Europe for a few years. Changed his name again, packed away all the evidence of his past as a war hero. He travelled with an acrobat troupe for several years. Learning the craft, working on his balance, coordination. He told himself that he did it to get a fresh start, away from the blood and dirt and mud and claustrophobia of the battlefield. He did it to be a better killer. He ended up in Thailand. He spent years there, studying with the kickboxers and martial masters. Learning their discipline and training regimens. He told himself he did it to learn focus, control. To learn how to tame that rage within him. He did it to be a better killer.

That's what he was. Whatever trappings he put on it, however many people he managed to help, he was a killer. Pure and simple.

The miles tore past under his tires. His mind drifted through the decades. He'd lived in three centuries now. Every moment of the past hundred and forty-three years worked through his mind over and over again in chaotic flashes as the next three hours passed.

Snow was deep on the roads when they arrived at Our Lady of Victory Basilica. Tommy pulled up against the curb. The tail of the Jag stuck out at an oblique angle. Tommy didn't care. He jumped out and ran toward the offices. Allison pulled up behind him and quickly caught up.

By the time he got to the door, Tommy could tell something was wrong. The door was shut, but there was damage by the knob. It looked like it had been kicked in, then put back in place to make everything look normal from the street.

Tommy pulled his revolvers. Allison reached into the back of her pants and pulled a .45. She looked at him and nodded, stepping a couple feet back from the door. Tommy backed up and put his foot into the door. It swung open with no resistance. Tommy almost fell forward. He entered the dark hall and pointed his guns to the right. From his time staying here recovering, he knew the layout of the building.

About twenty feet down the hall, there was a doorway leading to the stairs. The stairs led to the second floor and Father Daniel's office. Allison and Tommy made their way slowly down the hall, checking the doors. The whole place was dark. All the doors were locked. Tommy opened the hallway door and stepped through, moving slowly and keeping his pistols trained on the stairwell above him.

When they reached the top of the stairs, Tommy stopped for a moment. He listened. Nothing. No sound. He opened the door and checked the hall in both directions. He saw a light coming from the far end of the hall. Father Daniel's office. The door was open.

Tommy broke into a run. It was wrong. It was all wrong. Father Daniel *never* left the door open. When he turned into the room, he saw chaos. Lamps were on the floor, chairs overturned, books and papers scattered everywhere.

Allison came in right behind him. She stood at the door, looking over the room. Tommy saw it the same time he did.

"Tommy!" She said.

He saw it. A pair of feet in house shoes sticking out from behind the big Oak desk. He ran around the desk. Father Daniel was laying there, his face covered in blood. Tommy felt for a pulse, but couldn't feel anything. He put his cheek next to Daniel's lips. He felt a little bit of warmth coming from them. Father Daniel was alive, barely.

Tommy heard a commotion in the hall. Running feet. Stomping. He looked at Allison. She nodded and stepped to the side of the door. A large man turned the corner into the room. Allison swung her gun at him, but the man caught it mid-swing and threw her across the room by her arm, throwing a left jab into her ribs as she crossed in front of him. Allison hit the wall hard, bouncing off and landing in a crouch on the floor. The man raised his fist to throw another punch as she raised her pistol.

That was when Tommy saw it. On the man's hand. A glint of metal. Brass. Brass knuckles. Beaux!

"Allison! Beaux!" Tommy yelled. She turned to look at him as Tommy stood up. Beaux stopped mid-stride. He looked at Tommy, confused.

"She's with us!" Tommy said.

Beaux saw Father Daniel on the ground. He glared for a moment at Allison, then crossed the room to Tommy.

"What happened to him?" Beaux asked.

"They came for information on us, on me and her." Tommy said. "He's alive, but we have to get him to the hospital."

Beaux picked up the elderly priest and cradled him in his arms, walking toward the door. "Who did this to him?" He said.

"I think I might know." Allison said. She was kneeling on the floor near the desk, holding something shiny. She handed it to Tommy.

He looked at the small object. It was part of a man's ring, broken. He could see red on the top, and part of what looked like a crest with cyrillic letters.

"It was Rasputin. He and his men did this." Tommy said.

The three made their way back downstairs with Beaux in the lead. He took the stairs two at a time going down and ran across the snow covered lawn. Allison was a step behind him.

"My truck." She said to Beaux. She clicked a button on the remote to unlock the SUV and opened the rear door.

Beaux set Father Daniel gently onto the back seat. Tommy came limping up behind them as Allison ran around the truck to get in the driver's seat.

"Beaux drives." He said. Allison and Beaux both stared at him for a moment.

"Beaux drives." He said again.

Allison handed the keys to Beaux as they passed in front of the trick. She hopped in the passenger seat. Tommy climbed into the backseat and checked Father Daniel's pulse again. It was there. Very faint.

Beaux slammed the truck into gear and spun the tires as he pulled away from the curb. The SUV went sideways as he turned the first corner. Once he'd straightened out, he regained control.

The trip to Mercy Hospital should have taken about two minutes. Even with the snowy roads, Beaux got them there in less than a minute. He slid to a stop at the emergency entrance and jumped out, running around the truck to the passenger side rear door.

Tommy had already climbed out. Beaux grabbed Father Daniel and started yelling for a doctor. As soon as the desk nurse saw the large man carrying an elderly and clearly badly beaten man, they entire emergency department jumped into action. A gurney was brought out. Father Daniel was taken from Beaux's arms and rolled into triage. They tried to stop Beaux from following. Tommy came through the doors moments later and grabbed Beaux before he could throw a punch at an orderly.

"You need to talk to them, Beaux." Tommy said.

"I need to be in there with Father." Beaux replied. He had tears in his eyes.

"You need to tell them who he is. You know more about him than I do, you spent time with him. Tell them. Give them his patient history." Tommy said. He was holding Beaux's arms. Making Beaux look at him.

"Yeah. You're right. They need to know who he is." Beaux said. He turned away, then turned back to Tommy, leaning in close. "Someone's gonna pay for this." He said, then walked over to the nurse.

Tommy sat down in the waiting room. Allison had stayed outside to park the truck. She'd be in in a couple of minutes. This wasn't going to end well. All three of them were wanted fugitives. In a few minutes, this whole place would be swarming with police. The beating of a priest would bring everyone in. They had to keep their cool. Tommy took a deep breath. The air in the hospital felt cold in his lungs. He lowered his head to pray. He couldn't remember the last time he had.

"Mr. McKinney?" A female voice said.

Tommy looked up, shocked. A nurse was standing in front of him with a clipboard.

"Yes. I'm Mr. McKinney." He said.

"Father Daniel told us your name. He was conscious for a few minutes. He wanted to give you a message." She said, looking cautiously around the room.

"What did he say?" Tommy said, standing.

"He told the doctor to tell you, but they're on their way to surgery with him now." She looked around again.

"What did he *say?*" Tommy asked again.

"He said: *Tell Thomas I said nothing.*" She said, looking around the room a third time.

"Thank you." Tommy said.

"Your friends are upstairs in the surgery ward. I can tell you how to get there if you'd like to join them or," she said, not looking him in the eye. "I can stitch up that wound in your leg.". It was almost under her breath. She was staring at Tommy's left leg.

Tommy looked down. He hadn't realized that he'd torn the stitches in his leg. There was blood on his pants.

"Just get me a quiet place. I can stitch it myself. How long have I been sitting here?" Tommy said.

"About half an hour. Mr. Lafontaine and the woman with him tried to get you, but you wouldn't move." She said.

"Oh, I was praying." Tommy said. What the hell was going on? He just lost half an hour. On top of that, this nurse knew his name, knew Beaux's name. And why wasn't the hospital crawling with cops?

The nurse nodded. She led him to and exam room in the back and gave him fresh gauze and a suture kit. He'd torn every stitch in his leg. He hadn't even felt it. It didn't take long for him to sew it back together, but it was going to be an ugly scar. Tommy put the fresh gauze on the wound and got redressed. There was just a small spot of blood on his pants, but they were dark grey, and no one would notice unless they looked close.

Tommy made his way up to the surgery ward. Beaux was sitting by himself in the waiting room. He stood up when Tommy walked in.

"He's still in surgery." Beaux said. Tommy looked at him. It had been less than a year since Tommy had seen him last, but Beaux looked old. Worn, tired.

"Any idea?" Tommy asked.

"Well, punctured lung, perforated kidney and liver. Multiple broken bones. Possible heart attack. They worked him over, Tommy. Probably for a long time." Beaux looked at the ground.

"We're going to find them, Beaux. We're going to find them and make them pay. Just like last time. Where is Allison?" Tommy said.

"Her? Somewhere. Couldn't seem to sit still. Said she felt *exposed*. Where the hell did you find her?" Beaux said.

"Pittsburgh. They experimented on her. They used a device to try and turn her into an assassin. Made her into a psychopath instead." Tommy said.

"Jesus Christ." Beaux said.

Tommy sat down and Beaux sat next to him. They stared at the wall in silence.

Hours passed. Allison wandered in and out. Other people came and went. Nurses, doctors, civilians. Some of them glanced at Tommy and Beaux as they passed. Everyone here had their own troubles, and couldn't worry about two strange men sitting silent in a waiting room.

Tommy barely noticed that they were even there until the nurse from the emergency room tapped him on the shoulder.

"Mr. McKinney?" She said.

Tommy sat up in his chair.

"Mr. McKinney, you might want to close your jacket." She said, looking at his chest.

Tommy looked down. His jacket had come completely open. His guns were in full view. He grabbed the front of his suit coat and buttoned one button, looking around the room.

"How long?" He asked.

"About five hours now. It's almost six in the morning now." She said.

"Nurse," Tommy said, leaning toward the woman, "why is everyone..."

"We got a phone call. Sister Marguerite called from the church." The nurse interrupted. "She said that the church had invoked sanctuary for the people who brought Father Daniel in."

"How did she know?" Tommy asked.

"As soon as we knew who he was, we called the church. Sister Marguerite answered, and said she'd been given specific instructions if this happened. Father Daniel left a letter." The nurse said.

"So where are the police?" Tommy said.

"They'll be called in the morning, hopefully this will all be cleared up by then. When they get here, they'll be told that Father had been dropped off and no one knew who dropped him off, or who he was." She smiled. It was a weak smile. A weak attempt. After an awkward moment, she walked away down the hall.

Tommy sat there for a moment, wondering on Good Sister Marguerite. Allison had reentered the waiting room while he was staring into space and was now sitting vaguely reading an out of date magazine.

A surgeon in scrubs walked into the room. Beaux sat up, then stood up as the man moved toward them. Tommy stood as well, leaving only Allison sitting in the waiting room.

"Mr. McKinney, Mr. Lafontaine?" The doctor said.

Beaux and Tommy looked at him.

"I have some bad news for you." The doctor said, looking at the floor. "We did everything we could, but Father Daniel's wounds were too severe. There was internal bleeding..."

The doctor kept talking, but all Tommy could hear was a distant ringing in his ears. It got louder and louder as he stood there. His knees felt weak. He looked around the room, but couldn't bring his eyes to focus on anything. His heart was in his throat. He couldn't feel his feet on the floor anymore. There was a distant rage. Undirected, uncontrolled. Pure rage. Sadness. A burning in his eyes. The world went foggy. He felt cold, then nothing, then a burning in his chest.

Everything came back. Tommy watched a movie of his own emotions passing through his mind, but couldn't feel any of them. He had to go. Somewhere. Anywhere. Not here, but not anywhere else.

In the distance he could see Beaux. He'd punched a wall and was being held back by Allison. Tommy watched it all, disconnected from time. It moved slow, it moved fast. It was stopping and jumping forward. The ringing in his ears got louder. He saw Allison shouting at him. Something had broken. He was out of time. Looking in through at window at reality.

Tommy pushed past the doctor and walked out of the waiting room. It felt like he'd wandered for hours when he found himself outside the hospital chapel. He opened the door and walked in.

The crucifix. Not a cross. A crucifix hung in the center of the room. Christ sacrificed for our sins on the cross. But for who's sins? Not his. No. God would never claim Tommy as one of His own. To the right stood the Virgin. She looked down at the world with pity. Sadness in her eyes. She looked at Tommy with sadness. He kneeled down in front of her, lowering his head. He remembered the tears. The tears he'd cried all those years ago, the day he'd heard that Mary and Seamus were dead. The tears that had turned to blood on the floor of that church in Dublin. Were they his tears? Or were they hers? Was the Virgin Mother crying that day for what was about to be unleashed on the world?

Today there were no tears. Tommy had no tears left. That part of him was broken. It was gone, replaced by scars and visceral bloodlust. Righteous anger supplanted by habitual aggression. It had taken time. It had taken years. But the man he'd been, his humanity, was gone. Thomas McKinney was just a killer.

Tommy walked back to the waiting room in a fog. He had no idea of how long he'd been gone. As he reentered the waiting room, Beaux stood up. He had a look in his eyes. A violent face Tommy knew only too well.

The three of them stood in a tight group, speaking quietly about what might come next. As they spoke, no plan was forming. They talked in circles. Even Allison seemed to be having difficulty thinking straight.

Beaux looked up from the conversation. His eyes widened. He looked as though he wasn't sure what to say.

"Oh, shit." Said Beaux.

Tommy turned around. The figure was in black. A long hooded cloak and simple sandals. His hands folded in his sleeves. He walked with an arrogance. Brother Marcus, the Inquisitor.

He walked up to Tommy and Beaux and stood there, silent. The three men stared at each other for several moments before Marcus spoke.

"Do you see, Mr. McKinney, what happens when you involve yourself in things you don't understand?" He said. "People die."

Tommy stepped up close to the monk.

"You had something to do with this, Marcus. You and your little Inquisition. You killed Father Daniel to keep him from talking about your secret and helping me. He didn't know anything." Tommy said.

"We didn't have anything to do with Father Daniel being attacked. I'm only here as a representative of the Church. We just heard this morning that Daniel had been attacked. I assume that had something to do with you. I know you're a wanted man now, Mr. McKinney." Brother Marcus said.

Tommy grabbed Marcus by the neck and drew one of his Colts. He pulled him across the room and into an unoccupied office down the hall. Marcus struggled against Tommy's grip, but he wasn't strong enough to break it. Tommy threw him against the wall and forced the pistol into his mouth, cocking the hammer.

"I know you had something to do with this. I had a feeling you and yours were somehow involved, and now I'm sure of it. You say you want to keep the devices from falling into the wrong hands, yet you try and stop *me*? There's a madman out there giving these things out and trying to find ways to make more!" Tommy screamed.

"Tommy!" A female voice yelled from the door. Allison and Beaux had come into the room. "Tommy, normally I'd be all for you killing him, but now's not the time. We've got about fifteen minutes before this place is full of cops." Allison said.

"If we get stopped now, we won't find Rasputin." Beaux added. He stepped forward and put his hand over the top of Tommy's gun, sliding his finger in front of the hammer.

Tommy pulled the gun out of the monk's mouth. Brother Marcus was breathing heavy.

"You're trying to keep those monsters a secret," Tommy said, "but it's already out. The government knows about them, and they're looking for them even now. They're looking for Merrick's Codex, they're looking for the Horrors."

Brother Marcus stared at him.

"That's impossible." He said. "That has been a closely guarded church secret for centuries.

Only a select few people in the Church even know that they ever existed, much less that they still may. And Merrick's Codex? That book is a myth. No watchmaker has ever written down all their secrets, it's practically against the rules. Men like Merrick feared the information falling into the wrong hands just as much as we do. I don't believe you."

Marcus looked at Tommy with a mixture of indignation and disrespect. He thought Tommy was lying about it.

"Oh, they know, just ask Allison here." Tommy said.

"They've know about the devices for a little over a century." Allison said. "I've seen documents going back to the early Eighteen Nineties talking about possible military uses for this new technology. They seem to have known all along."

"But... That's just not *possible*." Brother Marcus said, wringing his hands.

Allison opened the door and glanced out.

"Tommy, we've got cops." She said.

Tommy looked at Brother Marcus.

"You've been lucky so far. The next time I see you Marcus, I'm going to put a bullet in your head. Understand?" Tommy pressed the barrel of the heavy Colt against the monk's forehead. Marcus nodded.

Tommy holstered the gun and buttoned his jacket, walking out of the office behind Allison and Beaux.

They made it out of the hospital without a problem. The police were too busy interviewing the doctors and nurses to notice three pretty average looking people walking out. The three of them were silent on their drive back to the church.

There was no one there. The police hadn't arrived to start looking for a crime scene yet, and any nuns or priests who might have come by would be inside on such a cold morning.

"We need to find somewhere to stay." Tommy said as he opened the door to his Jag. "Find us a motel, somewhere low. Let me know where and stay there until I come back."

Allison nodded. "What are you going to do?" She said.

"We know who did this. We know Rasputin and his men have been in town, maybe still are. This was my town for long time," Tommy smiled. A dark smile. "I'm going to find out where." He hopped in the Jag and pulled away from the curb leaving Allison and Beaux to figure out the details.

CHAPTER 12

Same shitty bar. Same shitty crowd. Tommy watched from the outside. Lowlifes went in, lowlifes came out. This was where he'd watched Teddy Barnes all those months ago. Back when this all started.

Something was different now, though. Tommy was different. He walked in the front door and stood for a moment, his eyes adjusting to the dim glow.

No one seemed to notice that he was there. Tommy pulled a Colt and fired a shot into the ceiling the round echoed in the small room. Now everyone was looking.

"I'm looking for anyone who knows the people who attacked the priest last night." Tommy yelled. "Father Daniel was attacked at the Basilica. I want to know who did it."

He saw movement to his right. The bartender. The man pulled a shotgun from under the bar. Tommy aimed and fired, hitting the old man in the head before he could raise the gun.

"Now you know I'm serious." He said "Who attacked the priest?"

"Nobody here knows anything. Might as well go before you get hurt." The voice was gruff, male. Tommy looked in the direction of the sound. The man who spoke stood out. He was big, rough looking even for this crowd. Tommy walked over to his table.

"Yeah, I know." Tommy said. "Crook's Code and all that. Well, you'll soon find out that I don't give a goddamn about much." Tommy picked up a full mug of beer off the table and slammed it into the man's face. The thick glass shattered, knocked him backwards out of his chair.

"Now. Who knows something? Nothing goes on in this town without somebody in this bar hearing about it." Tommy pulled his other pistol and scanned the room again. Near the front door, behind him now, was a familiar face. Slicked-back dark hair. Young. The man he'd seen in Pittsburgh. The man who'd been following him.

Tommy took a step forward, but the man got out the door before Tommy was even close. He didn't look like one of Rasputin's men. Too sane looking, too normal. He was probably just a spy for Brother Marcus.

When Tommy turned back to the room, he saw a skinny guy in jeans and a t-shirt headed for the back door. Tommy fired a round into the door before the man could get to it. He stopped and put up his hands.

Tommy crossed the room in a few steps and grabbed the man by the collar.

"What do you know?" Tommy asked, pressing the barrel of the revolver under the man's chin.

"Nothing. I don't know anything, I swear!" The man was nearly crying.

Tommy glanced over his shoulder. There were people moving around. Tommy kicked open the back door and threw the man out first, shut the door behind himself.

The man fell in the alley. He was kneeling in the snow with his hands up.

"I swear, I don't know anything about the priest!" The man said.

"You know something." Tommy said, standing over the man. "Tell me what you know." He pressed the pistol to the man's head.

"Okay!" The man cringed as the warm steel pressed against his skull. "I got this buddy, old partner of mine."

"Go on." Tommy said.

"Well, he's good with locks. That's his thing. So the other day he comes into the bar bragging about this big score he got. How these guys paid him a bunch of money to break into a church. Paid him half up front. The job was supposed to be last night." the man said.

"The door was kicked in. What was he supposed to get?" Tommy asked.

"That's the thing. He wasn't supposed to get anything. He was supposed to make it look like someone broke in, make it look like the place had been robbed." The man said.

"Why?" Tommy asked.

"He didn't know! Seriously, he didn't know. He figured they were mob guys or something, wanted to send the priest a message." The man said.

"What's his name?" Tommy asked.

"Come on, man. I can't give him up!" The man pleaded.

"What is his *name*?" Tommy asked again, pressing the gun hard against the man's head and cocking the hammer.

"Jason!" The man screamed. "Jason Myers! If you got a pen and paper, I'll even give you his address!"

Tommy took his notepad and pen out of his pocket and handed it to the quivering man on the ground in front of him. The man handed them back to Tommy who glanced at the paper and slipped it in his pocket.

"Okay, I gave him up. He's the guy you want to talk to. Can I go now?" The man said.

"You're a scumbag and a rat." Tommy said, pulling the trigger. The man's body slumped over in the snow. Blood and brain and bone littered the narrow alley, staining the snow a horrid pink.

Tommy slid his pistol into the holster and walked around the building to the street.

As he crossed the street to his car, he heard a voice behind him.

"Mr. McKinney?"

It was quiet, an unassuming question. But he wasn't taking any chances. Tommy ripped his Peacemaker out of its holster and spun around.

The man who'd been watching him threw his arms in the air.

"Whoa! I'm unarmed!" The man said. "I just want to talk!"

"I've heard that before." Tommy said, keeping the gun trained on the man. "You work for Brother Marcus?"

"I assure you, I don't work for the Inquisition. My name is father Paul Simanski. I work for His Holiness, the Pope." The man said, pulling out what looked like an ID card, similar to the one he'd been issued in Baton Rouge.

Tommy heard a touch of accent in his voice. "Polish?" He asked.

"Originally. I've been in the Vatican for several years." The man said.

Tommy stepped forward, taking the man's identification. It was the same guy, everything looked real, but there was no way to really be sure. He kept his gun out, but lowered it.

"What do you want?" Tommy asked.

"It's not what I want, Mr. McKinney. It's the Holy Father. Please, can we get out of the street?" The man said.

Tommy let the man lead the way to the sidewalk.

"Okay, now talk. What does the Pope want from me now?" Tommy said.

"There's a problem in the Vatican. His Holiness still supports you in your quest to stop the spread of devices, but there's a complication." The man said.

"What is it?" Tommy asked.

"Well, your actions, Mr. McKinney. The Inquisition, The Jesuits, led by Brother Marcus, are trying to get the Pope declared unfit to lead the Church. They want to install one of their own in his place." The priest crossed himself.

"What does that have to do with me?" Tommy asked.

"They're using your actions, and the Pope's continuing support of you, as evidence that he is no longer fit." Father Paul was visibly upset.

"What actions? What have I done?" Tommy said.

"What have you done? You *just* killed a man! Then there's the whole business in Pittsburgh, the fact that you're a wanted fugitive, Baton Rouge. You're a murderer! What more reason do they need? Right now, His Holiness has enough support to maintain his position, and he has access to the Inquisition's secrets. It's lead to a stalemate."

"The Pope's political issues are no concern of mine. Why doesn't he just excommunicate the lot of them?" Tommy said.

"He can't. Marcus has too many supporters. The excommunication of an Inquisitor requires a majority vote of Cardinals. Right now, between the bad feeling your actions have created and the Jesuits' cunning, the Pope doesn't have the votes. They're threatening to reveal his support and protection of a murderer to the public if he doesn't step down. It's not like he can tell the world he did it to protect the world from magic devices." The priest said.

"Yeah, I suppose that wouldn't make him look very sane, would it?" Tommy handed the priest his ID.

"No, it wouldn't. If His Holiness is deposed not only will it throw the church into chaos and put a militant conservative on the Throne of Saint Peter, but you'll lose all the protection and support the church has been providing these past several months. You'll be exposed." Father Paul said.

"That's not much incentive. It's not like I've gotten that much help." Tommy said.

"Mr. McKinney, you have no idea how much help you've gotten. We could only hold the NSA off for so long, and we couldn't do anything once you kicked the hornet's nest." Father Paul stared at Tommy.

Tommy could see it in his eyes. This wasn't a normal priest. This wasn't a normal man. This man had seen things, and he was probably the one acting for Tommy in the Vatican.

"Who were you before you joined the church?" Tommy asked.

"GROM." Father Paul said. One word. Four letters. So much weight.

"Polish Special Forces. How long?" Tommy said.

"Ten years. I joined the church two years ago. After Iraq, after Afghanistan." The priest continued to stare at Tommy.

"Why did you join the church? Not a normal choice for a soldier." Tommy said.

"I joined the army straight out of seminary. I thought I could be a chaplain. Instead, I joined GROM. I spent ten years a soldier, then His Holiness called me." Father Paul said.

"The Pope called you himself?" Tommy asked.

"Yes." Father Paul said, leaning up against the cold brick wall and pulling out a cigarette. He offered one to Tommy, who accepted. "He'd heard through the grapevine about my graduating seminary and joining special forces. He said if I rejoined the Church, he had a special assignment for me."

Tommy lit his cigarette off the priest's lighter and took a long drag. "What was the assignment?" He asked.

"You." Paul said, smiling for the first time. It was a warm, natural smile. One soldier talking to another now.

"I'm your *assignment?*" Tommy asked.

"My only one.   Run interference, track sightings and information.   Listen for chatter. Basically, I've been your counter-intelligence for the past three years." Paul said, chuckling through the smoke he'd just exhaled.

"Well, thanks for having my back." Tommy said, looking at the tip of his cigarette. What can I do for the Pope?"

"If you want to help him, to repay his kindness, you have to stop. Stop now, before the Inquisition can make a solid link." Father Paul crushed out his cigarette on the wall, tearing up the filter and tossing the cotton filler in the air. "In fact," he said, turning and walking up the street, "it would be better if you disappeared entirely."

With that, Father Paul was gone. Tommy thought of following him, but the man was a ghost. He wouldn't be found unless he wanted to be. Tommy knew that now. He pulled his keys from his pocket and slid into the Jag, starting the engine and letting it idle for a few moments before pulling away from the curb, headed for Jason Myers' apartment.

The apartment was a few miles away, to the north.   Tommy thought about his conversation with Father Paul as he drove through the snow-covered streets. They'd been watching his back. After everything he'd done, the lives he'd ruined, the people he'd killed, this group of men had protected him. One of them, a man he cared about and accused of spying on him, had just died to protect him. Katrina died trying to stop Rasputin, trying to help Tommy. Scotty had died for helping Tommy. How many others had? How many had died to help him during the wars? Faces without names flashed before him. Young and old. Eliza Merrick, Katrina Liu, Scotty, Father Daniel. He'd put Beaux in danger. He didn't ask for their help. He didn't ask for anything. All he wanted was absolution. All he was looking for was a cure for his curse. He wanted to get square with God. What if he couldn't? What if he really was like Allison, an aberration that didn't belong in the world? Too dangerous to be allowed to continue? What if he was the chaos?

Father Paul had said it. He'd said it all in one simple sentence: *it would be better if you disappeared entirely.*

He pulled up at the curb outside the run-down apartment building with Father Paul's words still ringing in his ears. He made his way up the stairs and found the address. It wasn't a bad place, just low rent.

He thought about pulling his gun and kicking in the door, but something made him think twice, hesitate. He knocked on the door.

After a moment a twenty-something man with a close trimmed beard answered, opening the door just enough to see Tommy.

"Can I help you?" The man said.

"Jason Myers?" Tommy asked.

"Yeah, that's me. Who's asking?" Jason said.

"I'm Tommy McKinney. I'm here to talk to you about the break in at the Basilica." Tommy said.

He barely got the sentence out before the door slammed in his face. Tommy took a step back and put his foot into the door. Pain shot through his leg. *Fucking stitches!*

He stepped back again and slammed the door with his shoulder. Pain exploded across his chest. *Fucking stitches!*

Tommy stepped back a third time and pulled one of his Colts, firing three shots into the doorknob. Putting his weight on his bad leg, he kicked with the good one this time. The door offered little resistance. He stepped through into the small apartment. There were baby's toys scattered all over. Tommy walked through the house looking for the man. There wasn't a back door. These types of apartments didn't have balconies usually.

He ended up in the bedroom. He stood there for a moment in silence. There were pictures of a happy couple everywhere. Jason Myers and a woman. Another picture, larger than the others, featured the woman and a baby.

Noise came from the closet. Tommy tore the sliding door open to find Jason holding a long barreled shotgun. He grabbed the barrel and pulled man and gun out in one motion. Myers let go of the gun and kneeled on the floor.

"I swear to God, I didn't know they were gonna kill him. I swear to God!" Myers said.

"Who hired you?" Tommy asked.

"I don't know." Myers said.

Tommy pointed the long barrel of his Colt Peacemaker at the man's chest.

"I don't know, man. I really don't know!" Jason pleaded.

"You never met them, never saw them?" Tommy asked.

"No, I mean, yes. I met them. But there weren't any names." Jason said.

"Do you know who I am, Jason?" Tommy asked.

"No, I don't. I've never seen you before." Jason said.

"My name is Tommy McKinney. I'm a killer. That priest that died was a friend of mine. I am not in a good mood today." Tommy said.

"I didn't know they were gonna kill him. They never said anything about hurting the old guy." Myers said.

"Tell me what they looked like, Jason." Tommy said.

The lock-breaker didn't even hesitate. "There were two of them." Jason said. "One was tall and thin. Really nice suit. The other one was foreign. He had a long beard and a thick accent."

"What kind of accent?" Tommy asked.

"I don't know. Foreign. Maybe Russian. He was a really big guy. They just paid me to make it look like I'd broken in. I didn't even go inside. Once I'd worked the door over, they paid me and sent me home, I swear." Jason said.

"Did these two men say anything else? Anything at all?" Tommy asked.

"No. They barely talked at all. They told me what and when. I didn't even know they were going to be there." Jason said.

Tommy cocked his Colt and leveled the gun between Myers' eyes. The man closed his eyes.

"Please." Myers said. "I have a wife. I have a baby. Don't let them find me like this."

Tommy looked around the room again. The pictures. Baby pictures. He thought about Seamus. How many of the men he'd killed had been fathers? How many had wives they never came home to? How many children never grew up knowing their dads because of Tommy's guns?

He walked out of the room, leaving Jason Myers cowering on the floor. He was nothing. A tool. He was just a man. He didn't have to die. How many times had Tommy been wrong before?

He barely made it to the bottom of the stairs. He heard gunfire in his head. Eruptions. Fireworks. Wooden wheels on cobblestones. Seamus crying on that rainy night so many years ago. The screams of his wife as they shoved her into a cage. He shook his head. The noise wouldn't go away. Words in Russian. The screams of a teenage girl as bullets flew past her on a cold night in eighteen ninety-eight. A splash in water. He felt a bullet rip through his hand. He looked at that scar. The scar that had started all of this. His mark. The bullet wound Rasputin had given him that night. He heard the moans of dying men in trenches.

Tommy collapsed on the sidewalk. Words in German and Polish. British and Irish accents. Voices begging for their lives. Men crying for their mothers as he slit their throats. That Nazi torturer. The gurgling sound he made as Tommy slid a sharpened hook down his throat. The noise he made when Tommy pulled it out. Sirens. Modern sirens.

He opened his eyes. Police. Coming now. He stumbled to the Jag and climbed in. He'd forgotten that he'd just shot a door open. Starting the engine, he pulled away from the curb. He focused hard through the noise in his head. Had to drive slow. Had to be careful. A police car flew past him headed in the other direction as Tommy turned a corner a few blocks from the apartment.

He had to go somewhere. He didn't know where Allison and Beaux were yet, but he had to go somewhere. He was in Buffalo. It had been his home for decades, but he had no home here now. He had no home anywhere. There was nowhere safe. He'd be looking over his shoulder from now on. But he had to find somewhere to go now.

CHAPTER *13*

Tommy found himself headed south. His heart led him where it always did in difficult times: To the church. A short while later he pulled up and parked in front of the Basilica. There was crime scene tape on the office door. No cops anywhere he could see. Maybe inside, but they'd probably finished collecting evidence by now. There was probably one or two still here to act as guards and make sure nobody disturbed the scene, but they wouldn't worry about him if he stayed outside.

He stepped out of the Jag onto the snow covered lawn. The cold wind scraped against his face. No matter how long you were out in the cold, you never really adjusted to it. It wasn't that long ago that he'd walked out those doors determined to head south for a while, to let the heat of his last run-in with Rasputin cool down. He'd intended to come back, to rebuild what he'd had. He'd planned on getting Father Daniel's help.

Father Daniel. Tommy never asked the old priest to help him, to get involved as deeply as he did. The man saw it as a duty, as a holy mission to stop these people, to live up to Father Baker's instructions, to always give Tommy sanctuary.

But he did more than that. He took in Katrina. He got them both medical care. He tried to get her to safety. Then he tried to save Tommy. He tried to save his soul. He was so convinced that there was something of the man Tommy had been left in there somewhere that he was willing to risk his life to find it, to show it to Tommy.

How long ago had he lost his soul? He'd never thought to wonder about that. In all the years between that night on the canal and today, Tommy hadn't once thought about what exactly did happen to his soul. He'd forfeited to take revenge for Mary and Seamus. But the people who'd destroyed his family were dead and gone, a century ago now. There was no reason for it anymore. He couldn't pin down when he'd become obsessed with killing, with finding the next person to hurt. He couldn't pin down when he started not caring who it was.

Maybe that's what Father Daniel was trying to tell him, to show him. That there was no call for vengeance on the world anymore. That it didn't matter. That nothing Tommy did would ever make those people pay. He could only see the road in front of him. There were no turns for Tommy McKinney, only a straight, blood soaked road. Leave it to a priest to give his life to protect a life not worth saving.

Tommy turned around and looked at the cemetery. Katrina was buried out there somewhere. Soon, Father Daniel would be, too. He walked across the street and in among the gravestones. There were so many of them. So many names of the dead. Old stones mixed in with brand new ones. Marble of all colors and carved into every conceivable shape. Some of the graves dated back to the early twentieth century. He might have known those people. He might have known a lot of the people who were buried here.

He'd thought at one point, many years ago, of having Mary and Seamus moved from the graveyard in Ireland to this one, to be closer to them. But he was uncomfortable about having them so close, where they could see what he'd become. They had known him as a good, honest man. A farmer who told the truth and paid his debts and went to church on Sunday. A father who was going to teach his son how to make an honest way in the world. They didn't know him as a vengeful, angry man with nothing but death in his heart. A monster with blood in its eyes and a gun under each arm. He didn't want them to know. He also didn't want them buried so close to so many men he'd personally put in the ground. Tommy was never superstitious, but the thought of his wife and men he'd killed being in close proximity made him uneasy all the same.

He thought about all those names, all those gravestones. He couldn't even say which ones he'd killed. He'd forgotten so many of them, some he never knew. He wondered to himself who had killed more people in cold blood, himself or Rasputin. It was probably Tommy. Rasputin wanted to rule the world, Tommy wanted to burn it.

Now Tommy had another purpose. Another reason to kill. There was another reason to put bodies in the cemetery. He'd figured out over the years that if you looked hard enough, there was always a reason. This time, it was Father Daniel, it was Beaux and Allison. The last thing Father would want. But he'd gone too far now, and there was no way to square his debt anymore. No way to clean his slate. The only thing left was to cleanse the world.

Tommy's phone vibrated in his jacket pocket, pulling him out of his thoughts. Tommy pulled it out and checked the text. It was Allison.

An address and room number. They'd found a hotel on the east side of the city. He limped back to the Jag. For the first time in days, he felt like he had purpose again.

He tried not to think too much as he drove. The incident at Jason Myers' apartment had shaken him. He just looked at the city in the cold. Icicles hanging off of every horizontal surface, and even some of the vertical ones. Was the lake frozen? He didn't know. Sometimes it froze, sometimes it didn't. When it didn't freeze over, that's when you knew it would be a hell of a winter.

He remembered the blizzard. Buffalo had seen a lot of them, but for people who remembered it, there was only one that mattered. Nineteen Seventy-Seven. The year the world stopped. He remembered walking over cars on the city streets. People were leaving work by stepping out of second floor windows onto the snow. Nothing moved. The mayor came on every TV and radio station and told the citizens to *get a six pack and stay home*. That was why he loved this town. Just have a few beers and wait it out. It'll melt eventually. That was Buffalo. That was the diehard attitude that had died not long after, when the factories and steel mills started closing. When the union leaders started slinking out of town with people's hard-earned retirements. That was the city he loved. It was gone, too.

His phone rang. Not a text message this time. A call. Focusing on driving on the slick roads, Tommy answered without looking.

"Hello?" He said.

"Mr. McKinney, yes?" A heavily accented man's voice said.

"Yes." Tommy replied.

"Mr. McKinney. My name is Grigori Rasputin."

Oh, fuck.

"Hello, there." Tommy said, trying to stay casual.

"We haven't seen each other in many months, Mr. McKinney. Not since you killed my friends and burned down my foundry." Rasputin's voice wasn't what Tommy expected. He was relaxed. Not menacing. Calm like he was talking to a child.

"I should have killed you then, you son of a bitch. Why did you kill Father Daniel?" Tommy said.

"These are not nice words. Your friend the priest, ahh yes. Sad. But he would not tell me where you were, you see, and I very much wanted to know that. But as you see, I do have your phone number now. Your other friend, he is a monk like myself." Rasputin laughed. "Well, not so much like myself. I don't cry so much when I get broken finger! Him? He told me after only one finger!" He laughed again. A deep, honest belly laugh.

"I'm coming for you, Grigori." Tommy said.

"Yes. Thank you for reminding me. This is why I call. I have your friend the monk. I do not want to kill him, though. Might be bad to kill the next Pope, yes? I think it's better for everyone if I just kill you, and let him go." Rasputin said.

"Might be. But if I'm going, you're going with me, Grigori." Tommy said.

"You'll find I do not die so easily as you might think. But anyway. He lives, you die. You come to the old brick warehouse on Ganson Street. You know it, yes?" Rasputin said.

"I know it." Tommy said. He'd worked in the building as a mechanic for a little while in the late sixties. It was right on the canal.

"You be there. Nine tomorrow morning." Rasputin hung up.

Tommy threw his phone on the passenger seat of the car. He felt that rage again. That low, slow burning anger that couldn't be calmed by kind words. The engine roared and he sped through the city toward the hotel.

When he arrived, he saw no trace of Allison of Beaux. He pulled up in front of the run down, shabby little motel and went to the room they had listed in their text. He knocked on the door. No one answered. He waited a few moments, no sound from inside. He raised his hand to knock again.

The door swung open. Allison stood there, pistol leveled at his head. Beaux was right behind her, holding the doorknob. Tommy instinctively reached for his guns before realizing who it was.

"Get in here." Allison ordered.

Tommy walked through the door and Beaux shut it behind him.

"Were you followed?" She asked.

"No, not followed. I got an interesting phone call, though." Tommy said.

Allison sat down at the small desk. She started cleaning her Glock, a process she'd obviously started before he knocked on the door.

"Phone call from who?" Beaux asked. He was sitting on the bed, a pump shotgun sitting next to him. The news was on the TV. They were talking about Father Daniel.

"Rasputin." Tommy said.

Allison and Beaux both looked up. Tommy took off his jacket and sat in the only empty chair in the room.

"What did he say?" Allison asked.

"He has Brother Marcus. He wants me. Simple as that. Marcus for me." Tommy said.

"Let him die." Beaux said.

"That was my thought, too." Allison added.

"I had a better idea." Tommy said. "Rasputin got my number from Brother Marcus. He thinks that Marcus and I are friends, thinks that I care about him."

"It's a trap." Allison said.

"Yeah, it's a trap." Tommy looked at her. "But Rasputin will be there, and he thinks I'll walk in expecting a prisoner exchange. He doesn't know I could burn the building down with all of them in it and not give a shit."

"So get him caught in his own trap?" Beaux said.

"Exactly. He's meeting me in a building at nine tomorrow morning. No doubt there'll be guards everywhere. I know the building. If he's on the second floor, we can trap him there. End this thing once and for all." Tommy said.

"I want Rasputin." Allison said. Tommy and Beaux both looked at her. "I owe him for what he helped them do to me."

"No." Tommy said. "He's mine. A hundred and fifteen years I've wanted him." There were six of us on that dock. There are..." Tommy stopped. He thought about Eliza Merrick. She was somewhere out in the world now, she was still alive and the only thing standing between Brinson and Merrick's Codex, if it existed. "...two of us left now. Rasputin and me. This needs to end now." Tommy's tone wasn't final. It was funereal.

"Okay," Allison said, "but if he knows where Brinson is, I need to know. I missed my chance in Pittsburgh when I rescued you. I'm not going to miss it again."

"Okay." Tommy said.

"I'll back the truck up to the door. We've got some preparations to make if we're doing this in the morning." She walked out of the room.

"Tommy," Beaux said, "I want a shot at him."

"I know you do, Beaux. And if you get one, you get one. To be honest, I don't give a shit who kills him, as long as he dies." Tommy was lying. He hoped Beaux couldn't tell. He wanted Rasputin. The two of them started this, and the two of them should end it.

Allison opened the door. Her truck was backed up to the curb with the rear hatch open. She had a large black bag in her hand. Tommy took the bag from her and handed it to Beaux. They passed bag after bag into the room. There were seven or eight in total. Then came a few smaller cases and a collection of ammo boxes.

Once everything had been set in the room, Beaux stood looking at the pile of gear on the bed. "Were you planning a war?" He said.

"No," Allison responded, "fighting one." She started pulling things out of bags.

There were four M16s, five AK47s, and ten various pistols, mostly Glocks and Barettas. She opened another bag and revealed two semi-automatic shotguns, Several revolvers, and boxes of ammo.

It went on and on. Grenades of every description and make. Submachine guns, knives, tripwires, claymore mines. There was enough of an arsenal to overthrow a small country.

When everything had been laid out, they stood looking at her collection.

"I should have brought more." She said.

CHAPTER 14

The next morning they were sitting outside the abandoned building on Ganson Street early. Allison looked through binoculars from behind the hood of her SUV parked up the street. Tommy had left the Jag a little further down the road where its tuned engine and open exhaust wouldn't draw attention.

She turned around and kneeled down behind the truck where Beaux and Tommy were waiting.

"Well?" Tommy asked.

"There are guards everywhere." She said. "Three story building. No guards on the top floor, but I counted five on the second floor and nine on the first with another two standing outside the wooden double doors. They're all armed, AKs and rifles, possibly pistols. There's a couple of pieces of derelict machinery between us and them that we can use for cover."

"That's a lot of firepower for a prisoner exchange." Beaux said.

"He knows who he's dealing with." Tommy said. "Plus, he's working with Brinson and his NSA buddies. That means he knows about her particular skill set." He pointed at Allison. "Also, he knows damn well this isn't a prisoner exchange."

"We should go in quiet," Allison said, "keep them guessing until we get close and open up on them once we're in range. Keep the element of surprise until the last possible moment."

"Good plan. Solid." Tommy said. "Rasputin's no fool. He knows we're going to try and kill him, and probably everyone else. For him, he wants the control. He's not going to kill me until the last possible moment. He wants to make me suffer as long as possible."

"So you have a better plan?" Beaux said, looking at Tommy.

Tommy walked to the back of the SUV. He opened the rear gate and started digging in one of the bags until he found what he was looking for. Two grenades. He slid them into his jacket pockets.

"We're going to blow them out?" Allison asked.

"No, there's too many of them, and it's too big a building for that. We'd never be sure we got all of them." Tommy said. He turned and looked at Allison and Beaux. "Get ready." He said. "When you see my signal, move in."

Tommy walked as quickly as his wounded leg would carry him up the street away from the building.

Allison looked at Beaux. "Is he coming back?" She said.

"I don't think he plans to." Beaux said, looking to where Tommy disappeared up the street.

Moments later there was a roar like thunder from the direction Tommy had left in. The shiny silver Jag screamed up the street past them, careening over the curb and through the chain link fence that surrounded the building.

Beaux and Allison saw him go by and started moving. They ran up behind the machinery in the building's yard and started firing. Allison with an MP5 and Beaux with an M16.

Tommy fought to keep the car on course as he hit the wet, snowy gravel in front of the building. The tail of the powerful Jag swayed wildly as the rear tires spun, shooting stones in every direction. He saw flashes of gunfire from the windows of the building and the two guards standing in front of the double doors. Bullets pierced the thin steel skin of the Jag, tracing rows and uneven trails up to the windshield and across. Tommy ducked down behind the dashboard, holding the wheel steady with one hand, keeping the car pointed at those doors. Shards of glass sprayed the inside of the cab. He felt it embed itself in his hands and face.

There were two heavy thuds in quick succession. The two guards at the door. Tommy braced for what was coming.

The wooden door splintered over the front of the heavy car, the hinges pulling out of the wooden frame. The car bounced a couple of times, all four tires leaving the ground. There was a huge noise as the car slammed into something solid. Tommy was thrown into the steering wheel as the Jag came to rest. Pain shot through his body. His wounded shoulder and leg screamed. He heard gunfire as he forced open the door of his ruined car.

Tommy rolled sideways out of the car. Bullets bounced through the rubble all around him on the concrete floor. Tommy fired at the first person he saw, drawing his Peacemakers and shooting for the chest as the man raised his AK47 to fire.

He realized suddenly that not all the guards were firing at him. There were men standing in the windows shooting out. Beaux and Allison were firing into the building. Tommy dropped another two. He saw three guards fall as he moved toward them, victims of Allison's supernatural aim.

Looking up over the car, Tommy saw stairs leading up. Rasputin wasn't down here. The room was open. Tommy would be able to see him. He had to be on the top floor, where there weren't any guards.

He ran for the stairs. The remaining guards were preoccupied with the constant rain of lead coming from Allison and Beaux outside. No one even tried to stop him as he climbed the stairs at a run.

Outside, Allison and Beaux were aiming their shots. They tried to keep the guards on both floors occupied, to give Tommy a fighting chance in there. There was too much open space between them and the building to get in there and help him. All they could hope to do was keep the guards off them.

Gradually the gunfire from the building tapered off until only one guard was still alive to shoot. Allison took the M16 from Beaux, trading him the less accurate MP5. She took a long, deep breath and aimed at the window where the last guard was shooting on the second floor. He had ducked down behind the brick wall below the window. She sat silent, waiting. The moment that passed seemed to take minutes. She saw the barrel of the AK47 rise in the window. Closing her eyes, she pulled the trigger.

The wood frame of the window exploded. Beaux saw the man's hands flailing in the air, dropping the AK47. Just the top of his head was visible falling backward. She'd shot him in the head through the window sill.

Allison opened her eyes and looked at Beaux. "Let's go." She said. Her voice was calm, level. She might as well have just pressed enter on a keyboard. She stood up and started toward the building with Beaux close behind. They had only gotten a few feet on the other side of the derelict machinery that had been their cover when a strange sound started echoing off the grain silos and industrial structures around them. The sound of rotors.

A small helicopter buzzed directly overhead, less than a hundred feet off the ground. Allison ducked down. Beaux followed her lead. The noise of the helicopter was followed by the sound of trucks behind them. They both turned to see five black SUVS pull into the yard, cutting them off from Allison's truck.

A group of men in bulletproof vests jumped out of the trucks. Allison fired at burst from the M16 hitting one of them and forcing the rest to dive for cover behind their vehicles. The men returned fire with assault rifles and pistols, pinning Allison and Beaux behind the machinery with a twenty yard open run to the building.

Tommy heard the sound of a helicopter over the building. Gunfire erupted outside as he cleared the second floor. He couldn't worry about Beaux and Allison now. They could take care of themselves. Looking into the second floor as he passed, he saw the bodies of guards lying around the room, mostly by the windows. Yeah, Allison and Beaux could take care of themselves.

He kept running up. The stairs ended in a wooden door with a frosted glass window set into it. He couldn't hear if there was any movement inside over the noise of the helicopter. It seemed to have landed on the roof of the building. Probably Rasputin's escape plan.

Tommy pulled out his second pistol, cocked both guns, reared back and kicked the door in. The room was an empty, hollow shell. Rough wooden floorboards were coated in a layer of dust. In the center of the room stood a black-robed figure next to a chair. Rasputin. The chair had another robed man in it. His face was beaten bloody, and his hands and legs were bound. Brother Marcus. Rasputin raised a revolver and pointed it at the beaten monk, cocking it.

"Mr. McKinney," Rasputin said, "we always seem..."

Tommy didn't stop moving. He raised the half empty gun in his left hand and fired one shot. It hit Marcus in the head, throwing him over backwards in the chair. Rasputin pointed his pistol at Tommy, a shocked expression flashing across the Russian's face. Tommy cocked his left pistol again and pointed it at Rasputin.

The monk fired. Rasputin's haphazard shot hit the floor at Tommy's feet. Tommy kept moving forward, but the shot was close enough to make him loose his aim. Before he could level his shot again, Rasputin had run for a flight of stairs in the back of the room. The stairs to the roof.

He was out of sight in less than a second. Tommy moved as fast as he could to catch up. By the time he reached the roof, Rasputin was nearly in the helicopter. Tommy bolted for him, catching him just as he was stepping into the small craft.

On the ground, Allison and Beaux were ducked down behind the machinery, trying to protect themselves from the agent's continuous fire. Allison was ducking in and out of the equipment, firing back when she could. They were both very low on ammo. Allison had one clip left, and Beaux was down to half of one on the MP5. They couldn't keep this up for long before the agents would realize that they were out of bullets and just overrun them.

Allison looked at Beaux. He had fear in his eyes. If they took him, they'd experiment on him, too. She knew who his father was, even if he didn't.

"When I give the signal, run. Run as far and fast as you can. Got it?" She said.

Beaux stared at her, wide eyed.

"Do you understand me?" She yelled.

Beaux nodded. He set the MP5 on the ground.

Allison picked up the gun and tossed it over the machinery. She dug in her pocket, pulling out her car keys. Then she tossed the M16 alongside the MP5.

"I'm unarmed!" She yelled. "I'm coming out!" She put her hands up with the car keys in her right hand. Slowly she stood up, exposing herself to the agents. They didn't fire.

"When I give the signal." She said again. She didn't look down to see if Beaux was ready. A pair of agents started to move forward, keeping their guns pointed at her. Allison smiled. She pushed a button on her truck remote. The SUV exploded into a fireball behind the agents. Beaux broke off in a sprint headed for the street. The agents, shocked by the blast, some wounded or on fire, were too preoccupied to notice.

Allison walked out in front of the machinery and kneeled down, still smiling. The agents moved in quickly on her.

Tommy dragged Rasputin out of the helicopter. The big Russian, caught off balance, fell on top of Tommy. Tommy dropped the pistol in his right hand. Rasputin rolled over and started throwing punches, landing pretty much every one on Tommy's head.

Tommy managed to get his knees between him and Rasputin and push him off. Tommy rolled backward, raising his remaining gun to fire. Rasputin was too close already. He swung at Tommy's arm, knocking the gun from his hand and sending it sliding across the roof.

A huge explosion rocked the building, throwing both men off their balance. An orange ball of flame cleared the roof and extended a hundred feet further in the air. Tommy glanced over to see Allison on her knees and Beaux running for the street.

Rasputin kept throwing punches. Tommy blocked and dodged as best he could, getting in a few shots of his own, but he was being backed up toward the edge. Just feet from the edge, the Russian lunged. Tommy had no time to sidestep or redirect. He took the impact in his chest and fell to the ground with his head hanging off the building.

Rasputin continued to punch. He reached for Tommy's throat, using his shoulder for leverage. Tommy screamed in pain as the huge hand gripped his wounded arm. Rasputin smiled. A sick, grisly smile. He squeeze tighter.

Tommy hit him in the stomach, pulling and grabbing at his robes as Rasputin tried to choke the life out of him. Finally, Tommy managed to again get his feet on the Russian's stomach and push. He was heavy, but Tommy had the leverage.

Rasputin rolled back several feet, coming up on his feet. He'd landed next to Tommy's right hand gun. He lifted the gun and fanned the hammer, firing all six shots into Tommy's chest.

Tommy stood looking at the blood running from his heart. He pressed his hand into the fresh, warm redness. Pulling it away, he looked at the blood running off it. He stepped back to the edge of the building, his heels hanging over the freezing water of the canal. He raised his face to Rasputin, a grim, bloody, arrogant smile spreading across his lips.

Tommy raised his right hand. Hanging from his middle finger were two small rings with straight pieces of metal hanging from them. Grenade pins.

Rasputin stared for half a second, then tried to dig into the multiple folds of his monk's robe. Tommy's eyes closed. His knees failed. He fell backward off the building. He heard the simultaneous explosion of two frag grenades. He saw Father Daniel. Katrina Liu. Mary and Seamus smiled at him from a sunny field, walking hand in hand toward him. He felt in the distance the cold water hit his body. Everything went black.